"Young children remember more than we think."

Eli looked at the woman sitting beside him with some surprise and a new respect. That made sense. It was the best explanation he'd ever heard— far more simple and true-sounding than all the gobbledygook he'd heard from that *Englisch* doctor.

"That's so. I need a woman who'll understand that and not be harsh when Leah gets upset over silly things. Do you think this nanny you know would be a good fit?"

"*Ja.* I do."

Eli felt a wave of relief. Maybe this was going to work out after all.

"*Gut.* Leah's four now, so I've a couple of years before she starts school. I'll need somebody to watch her while I'm working, and I'm willing to pay well for the right person. So who do you have in mind?"

Trudy had been listening attentively, her brow crinkled, but at his question, she flushed. She clamped her hands together in her lap, straightened her shoulders and looked him in the eye. "Me."

Laurel Blount lives on a small farm in Georgia with her husband, David, their four children, a milk cow, dairy goats, assorted chickens, an enormous dog, three spoiled cats and one extremely bossy goose with boundary issues. She divides her time between farm chores, homeschooling and writing, and she's happiest with a cup of steaming tea at her elbow and a good book in her hand.

Books by Laurel Blount

Love Inspired

A Family for the Farmer
A Baby for the Minister
Hometown Hope
A Rancher to Trust
Lost and Found Faith
Her Mountain Refuge
Together for the Twins
A Family to Foster
The Triplets' Summer Adventure

Hickory Springs Amish

The Amish Widower's Surprise
Trusting the Amish Farmer
A Courtship for the Amish Nanny

Visit the Author Profile page at LoveInspired.com.

A COURTSHIP FOR THE AMISH NANNY

LAUREL BLOUNT

If you purchased this book without a cover you should be aware that this book is stolen property. It was reported as "unsold and destroyed" to the publisher, and neither the author nor the publisher has received any payment for this "stripped book."

ISBN-13: 978-1-335-62149-8

A Courtship for the Amish Nanny

Copyright © 2026 by Laurel Blount

All rights reserved. No part of this book may be used or reproduced in any manner whatsoever without written permission.

Without limiting the exclusive rights of any author, contributor or the publisher of this publication, any unauthorized use of this publication to train generative artificial intelligence (AI) technologies is expressly prohibited. Harlequin also exercises their rights under Article 4(3) of the Digital Single Market Directive 2019/790 and expressly reserves this publication from the text and data mining exception.

This is a work of fiction. Names, characters, places and incidents are either the product of the author's imagination or are used fictitiously. Any resemblance to actual persons, living or dead, businesses, companies, events or locales is entirely coincidental.

For questions and comments about the quality of this book, please contact us at CustomerService@Harlequin.com.

® is a trademark of Harlequin Enterprises ULC.

Love Inspired
22 Adelaide St. West, 41st Floor
Toronto, Ontario M5H 4E3, Canada
www.LoveInspired.com

HarperCollins Publishers
Macken House, 39/40 Mayor Street Upper,
Dublin 1, D01 C9W8, Ireland
www.HarperCollins.com

Printed in Lithuania

Hope deferred maketh the heart sick:
but when the desire cometh, it is a tree of life.
—*Proverbs* 13:12

For Nettie Holloway, whose memory I cherish dearly
and whose faith and kindness inspires me still

Chapter One

She shouldn't complain—but, oh, she wanted to!

Trudy Schwartz plopped another washbasin of freshly picked pears down on the kitchen table. Ever since lunchtime she'd been plucking ripe fruit from the big tree outside— and sneaking wistful peeks into the Christian romance novel she'd tucked in its branches.

The only romance she'd ever experienced had been between the pages of the books she borrowed from the town library, and usually she enjoyed them. But today the sweet love story just made her own situation harder to bear.

Outside this steamy kitchen the Amish families of Hickory Springs, Tennessee, were enjoying a beautiful Saturday afternoon, the first day of September.

September.

Trudy had been renting a room from matchmaker Susie Raber for three whole months, and there was still no real-life romance in sight.

She'd tried to be patient, she really had. But she'd be twenty-nine on her next birthday and still unmarried in a community where women often became grandmothers in their forties. Time was ticking by, and the only thing Susie seemed to care about was concocting new recipes for the bakery where she worked.

Today, though, she'd set her baking aside to focus on preserving her bounty of pears. The water bath canner was bubbling on the stove, and Susie hummed as she peeled fruit for pear preserves. She smiled at the dappled green fruit heaped inside the washbasin.

"Such a *gut* year for pears," she said. "You and I have our work cut out for us."

Trudy smothered a sigh. She didn't think pears were that exciting. On the other hand, Susie was so cheerful and kind it was impossible not to love her.

"After working all week at the bakery, I'd think you'd be tired of cooking."

Susie laughed. "I never get tired of cooking. That's why I took the job at Smucker's Bakery in the first place."

"Just like I'm a nanny for the Johnsons because I love children." She should have stopped there, but she couldn't resist adding, "I've always prayed that one day I'd be blessed with some little ones of my own. Of course," she murmured, "I'll need a husband first."

Susie shot her a warning look as she dropped a long green peel into the scrap bowl. "Please don't start, Trudy."

"I'm sorry, Susie, but I've been living here for months. I'd hoped by now…" No need to finish that sentence. Susie knew perfectly well what Trudy hoped.

"Hoping is one thing. Expecting is another." The older woman dropped the peeled pear into a basin of salted water. "I know I have a reputation for making matches, and I do like the fun of helping lonely folks pair up. But I've never made any promises, not to you nor to any other *maidel* I've rented my spare bedroom to."

"*Nee*, you haven't," Trudy admitted as she unloaded the new pears into a colander for rinsing. "It's just…all my friends are married now, and my sisters and brothers, too."

Not only married, but busy with young growing families. Everywhere she looked these days another promising bump was rounding out a friend's apron. Trudy tried not to be envious, but it was hard when her own arms and heart felt so empty.

Susie's expression softened. "I understand, but right now there just aren't many bachelors in Hickory Springs close to your age." She slanted a teasing look at Trudy as she picked up another pear. "Although I did hear Ephram Miller's looking for a second wife."

"Ephram Miller?" Trudy made a face. "I know I'm a little older than most *maidels* who come to you for help finding a husband, but I'm hoping for more than a whiskered widower old enough to be my *grossdaddi*."

Susie laughed. "Then you'll have to be patient. Realistic, too. Life doesn't work like those romance books you like to read. The perfect fellow isn't likely to come riding up out of the blue and sweep you off your feet."

"I know." Trudy's cheeks flushed pink. The truth was, she'd secretly hoped that's exactly what would happen after she moved in with the town matchmaker. That for once in her lonely life, a man, a nice, kind, pleasant-looking man, would fall in love with *her*. "I'm being realistic. I've just been waiting so long that I've started to worry I'll never get married."

"Worrying does no good," Susie reminded her matter-of-factly. "Besides, so what if you never find a husband? Being a Good Apple Girl isn't the worst thing in the world."

A Good Apple Girl? Trudy's heart plummeted to her shoes. A Good Apple Girl was one who never married, called so because their Amish community kindly said that the sweetest apples were often left unpicked on the very tip-top of the tree.

"Is that really what you think, Susie? That there might be no *mann* out there for me at all?" Trudy held her breath as she waited for the answer.

"I don't know what *Gott* has planned for you, Trudy." Susie offered her a sympathetic smile. "What I do know is that He wants us to be content and cheerful wherever He puts us, even if it's not where we'd like to be. Cheer up. If the Lord has a husband set aside for you, He's sure to send the fellow your way sooner or later." The older woman winked. "In the meantime, those pears won't pick themselves."

"*Nee*, I suppose not." With a sigh, Trudy picked up the empty washbasin and headed back outside. The autumn afternoon was warm and bright, but after her conversation with Susie, Trudy found little comfort in the balmy weather.

So Susie believed Trudy might end up a Good Apple Girl. That was discouraging, given that Susie's specialty was finding husbands for hard-to-match *maidels*. Hadn't she matched up Lilah Troyer with storekeeper Eben Miller? Nobody in town had seen that coming, but they made a sweet couple, and Eben was obviously head over heels in love with his new bride.

And what about Anna Speicher? Anna had told Trudy more than once that she never planned to remarry after her husband Henry's death, but somehow Susie had worked it out, and now Anna was happily married to produce farmer Jeremiah Weaver. And the way Jeremiah looked at his Anna, as if he couldn't believe what a blessed man he was...

No man had ever looked at Trudy that way—not once. And Anna hadn't even *wanted* a husband.

Trudy twisted another pear off the tree. It seemed so unfair. Anna's and Lilah's unexpected romances were why she'd moved here from her parents' home. She was tired of waiting for a fellow to take notice of her. Surely, she'd thought, she couldn't be any harder to match up than Anna and Lilah.

But maybe she was, and she was running out of time. Her nanny job with the Johnsons had shifted to part-time, so she couldn't afford to live at Susie's for much longer.

Her parents were happy at the idea that she might be moving home soon. Her six siblings were all married and living on their own now, and *Mamm* had mentioned at church last week how much she missed her daughters' help with the canning and preserving. *Daed* was processing a steer in October, and her parents clearly believed Trudy would be home by then and able to pitch in with the work involved in putting up the fresh beef for the winter.

She loved her parents, and of course she never minded helping them. But if that happened—if she had to go back home still single—she'd be a Good Apple Girl forever. She just knew it.

She stepped behind the tree and picked pears off the sagging branches, thumping the fruit into the wash pan. Her gaze caught on the paperback she'd tucked among the leaves, and she sighed.

If she moved back home, she'd have to give up the library books as well. *Mamm* had never approved of them. And then the only sparkles of romance she'd ever experienced would fade out of her life forever.

"Gott," she whispered sadly, "if you do have a *mann* for me, I wish You'd hurry up and send him along."

The rattle of a buggy turning into Susie's driveway made her freeze, one hand cupping a pear. Slowly, she tugged it from its branch and edged around the tree trunk to peek through the leafy branches.

A buggy—a nice, family-sized one—rolled into the drive. A man was driving, a little blonde girl perched beside him on the seat. She was wearing a light blue Plain dress and looked to be about four years old. She had her finger in her mouth and was looking around Susie's yard curiously.

The man next to her appeared to be in his thirties, with dark brown hair, ruffled in the breeze, and a lean face set in stern lines. He sat stiff and straight on the bench seat, as if he was mad about something. But when the little girl spoke to him, he glanced down at her, his expression softening in a way that caught at Trudy's heart.

Was he her *daed*? *Nee*, the man had no beard. That meant he wasn't married.

Trudy sucked in a quick breath. A thirty-something-year-old Plain man who wasn't married? That wasn't something you saw every day, especially not in Hickory Springs.

She squinched her eyes tight. *"Denki, Gott,"* she murmured fervently. Then she opened her eyes, gathered her courage and stepped out from behind the tree.

The movement caught the man's eye. He studied her as he slowed his horse to a stop, his face hardening into its earlier grimness.

"Is this the matchmaker's house?"

He was looking for a matchmaker? Trudy's already pounding heart did a hopeful somersault.

"Ja, it is." She took a few steps closer. The man's eyes were hazel-brown, with little flecks of green in them. Real nice eyes, she thought—or they would be if they looked a bit more friendly. *"Vass vitt du?"* she managed to ask.

"What do I want?" The man made an irritated noise. "I'm asking for the matchmaker, ain't so? What do you think I want?"

"I—I—" The brown-haired woman's eyes widened at his rudeness, and Eli felt a jab of familiar guilt.

He'd spoken too short and hurt her feelings. He'd not meant to. It wasn't her fault he'd been prodded here by a pair of interfering bishops who believed a little girl could only be raised properly by a woman.

He looked down at Leah. His four-year-old niece looked up trustingly, and the resolve in his chest strengthened.

He'd promised his sister—and himself—that he'd do whatever it took to keep Leah safe with him. And he would. Even if it meant talking with this matchmaker, who was staring at him now as if he'd turned green.

Small wonder. He'd never been any *gut* at talking to people, women particularly. He always put a foot wrong somehow.

"Sorry," he muttered. "I didn't mean to be rude."

He never did. But he usually was.

"That's all right," the woman assured him.

She was younger than he'd expected. The Hickory Springs bishop had described the matchmaker as a middle-aged widow with plenty of experience matching folks up. This woman was no schoolgirl, but he wouldn't call her middle-aged, either. And there was something strangely innocent about her that made her look even younger…something in her eyes. They were a clear spring green, just the shade of the pear she clutched in her hand, and she was smiling at him—a great big smile.

This young matchmaker must have a long list of women looking for husbands, Eli thought glumly. She sure looked happy to have him standing in her yard.

He, on the other hand, wasn't happy at all. He'd much rather have been back in his *kossin*'s furniture store, getting his woodworking tools sorted out. Or finishing the unpacking and settling in their new home with Leah. He'd rather have been anywhere but here, but after his meeting with the bishop, he'd had little choice.

"So," the young woman went on hopefully. "You want to get married?"

Eli set the brake—and his jaw—and prepared to get out of the buggy. He stayed silent because there was only one way for him to honestly answer her question.

Nee, he didn't want to get married. He'd given up on the whole idea after Mary Hershberger had turned him down flat twelve years ago.

He'd been nineteen then, and his parents had been dead five years. He'd been working hard, rebuilding his *daed*'s furniture business and was finally making enough money to move out on his own.

And not a moment too soon. He'd been worried sick about his younger sister. Living with his strict *aent* and *onkel* had made Eli—already a loner—grow even quieter and more solitary. Abby was a different story. His sister had seemed determined to shipwreck her life with drinking and wild *Englisch* boys, in spite of the strictness of their adopted household. Or maybe because of it.

So, he'd figured, a bit reluctantly, that the *schmaert* thing to do would be to marry Mary. Mary was Abby's age—two years younger than he was—and the two had been friends in school. Other girls had pulled away from Abby when she'd refused to be baptized, but Mary had continued to be kind.

Eli had never taken any special notice of Mary before, but he'd always liked her. She'd been widowed only four months after her marriage, and, like Eli, had been coming under some pressure to marry. After the wedding, Abby could move in with them, and then maybe she'd settle down.

He'd thought it a very sensible plan. But Mary had said no.

"I like you, Eli," she'd said gently. "But I don't love you, and I couldn't be happy married to a fellow I didn't love. You wouldn't be happy, either. You're happiest alone, working in your shop. You always have been."

Two weeks later, Abby had run away, vanishing into the *Englisch* world. He'd only laid eyes on his sister once since then—the day she'd shown up unannounced, a sad desperation in her eyes, to leave her two-year-old daughter in his care.

That day had changed everything. Leah had changed everything.

Eli jumped from the buggy to the ground, and Leah stepped into his arms, clinging to him tightly as he swung her down. The feel of her little fingers digging into his shirt strengthened his resolve.

He'd told Abby he'd take care of her daughter, and bishops or no bishops, he planned to keep his word. Even if he had to get married to do it.

He faced the woman. "I'm Eli Mast. And I'm guessing you'll be Susie Raber?"

"*Nee,* I'm Susie," another woman called from the house.

Confused, he glanced in that direction. A slender middle-aged woman stood on the back steps, drying her hands on a striped dish towel. "Can I help you?" she asked.

"He's looking for a matchmaker! I'm Trudy, by the way," the green-eyed woman told him with a smile. "Trudy Schwartz."

He wasn't sure what to say, so he picked Leah up and started toward the older woman. "The bishop sent me. I... uh... He thought you and I should talk."

"All right." The matchmaker's eyes sharpened with curiosity. "Come on in the house. I've got pears canning, but I can work while we have our chat. Is this your little girl?"

"She's my niece, but *ja*, she's mine to look after. Her name is Leah."

Susie nodded. "I see. Leah, it's very nice to meet you. Now, while your *onkel* and I have our little talk, would you like to help Trudy pick pears?" She smiled at Eli. "Trudy works as a nanny, and she's wonderful with children. That way you and I can speak plainly."

A shadow crossed Leah's face, and she tugged urgently on his hand. When he bent down, she whispered in his ear, "Can't I stay with you? Please? I'll be quiet and good."

Susie watched him, probably waiting to see if he'd give in and let the child have her way. He'd gotten sharp glances from women in Carroway, his hometown, for that more than once. It wasn't the Plain way to let a child coax her way out of obeying an adult.

But those women didn't understand how anxious Leah got when he wasn't nearby or when something was new or strange. She tried hard to do as he asked, but she got *naerfich* easily, no doubt from the chaotic time she'd spent with her mother before coming to him. That's what her doctor thought, anyway. The man had used a lot of big words and seemed to talk in circles.

But Eli hadn't needed big words to understand how Leah felt. People made him uneasy, too. Always had.

He was about to say that he'd rather Leah come in with him when the woman named Trudy walked up. She crouched on the grass, eye level with the little girl.

"Hello," she said with a smile. The woman had a generous mouth, so it was a big smile—too big to be pretty. But he had to admit, it gave her oval face a real friendly look. "I'm Trudy, and I'm picking pears off that tree over there." She pointed toward a laden tree, its branches bent nearly to the ground. "It's a big job for just one person. Do you think you could help me?"

Leah looked from the pear tree to Trudy, one finger in her mouth. She was thinking it over, Eli realized, and that surprised him. "Do I have to climb up the tree?" she whispered.

"*Nee*. You can pick the ones close to the ground." Trudy lowered her voice. "And I'll tell you a secret. If you duck through those branches, inside the tree by the trunk, you'll find a special place, like a little green room with pears hanging all over the walls."

Leah's eyes widened. "Really?" She looked up at Eli. "Can I go see?"

He was so surprised it took him a minute to answer. "*Ja*, go ahead."

Trudy took Leah's hand, and his niece went along as if she'd known the woman her whole life. Eli stared after them, unsure what to think. Leah had never taken to a stranger like that before.

"Well, come on." Susie sounded amused—and impatient. "I've got a canning kettle on the stove."

He followed her into a homey kitchen that smelled strongly of pears.

"So." Susie grabbed a pot holder and picked up the lid of the canning kettle to check on her jars. "You said Charley Coblentz sent you?"

"He did."

"That doesn't happen often—that the bishop sends someone my way. Usually it's when they need to get married extra quick or are having a lot of trouble finding a partner." She glanced up from the stove. "Which is it with you?"

Eli shifted his weight uncomfortably from one boot to the other. "I…guess it's the quick part."

"You guess?" Susie's brow crinkled as she set the lid on

the counter. "It's time to take out the jars," she explained. "Is it because of your niece? Are you finding it hard to care for her alone?"

"I'm here because of Leah, but not because I can't take care of her. I've looked after her for two years just fine." It annoyed him that the bishops assumed he couldn't look after Leah by himself. Sure, it had been hard to start with, but he'd figured everything out, hadn't he? "But the bishops think Leah needs a *mamm*."

"The *bishops* think so." Susie lifted an eyebrow. "More than one? I'm surprised even one bishop is involved in something like this. It's not usually something they'd concern themselves with, not so long as the child seems to be well looked after. And Leah does, at least as far as I can see. Unless..." She finished folding a towel on the table and returned to the stove. "Unless they got dragged into it somehow."

That wasn't exactly a question, but clearly she expected an answer.

"They were. At least, Jakob Hochstedler was. He's the bishop over in Carroway, Tennessee, where I grew up. And I guess I dragged Bishop Coblentz into it, although I didn't mean to."

"And who dragged in Jakob?"

"My *aent* and *onkel*. They want to raise Leah themselves." As the matchmaker used a pair of tongs to move the hot jars from the water to the waiting towel, he explained—with as few details as he could—what had happened with Abby. He watched the older woman's face closely, but her expression never wavered. If she disapproved of his sister's choices, she didn't show it—which was far better than most people managed.

So he went on to tell her how his childless relatives, upset that he wouldn't surrender Abby's daughter to them, had taken their appeal to the bishop. Jakob had suggested that Eli either find himself a wife or surrender Leah to Lora and Menno Mast to raise.

That, to Eli's way of thinking, wasn't any choice at all. Where was he going to find a woman to marry in such a hurry? It couldn't be just any woman, either. Not only would she have to put up with him—an awkward loner who couldn't seem to string two words together without putting his boot in his mouth—she'd have to be kind and patient with Leah, too.

For some reason, his mind flicked to the green-eyed woman outside. Leah seemed to like her well enough.

"I see." Susie cupped the bottom of a dripping jar with a dish towel as she moved it to the counter. "And you thought you'd sidestep the problem by moving to a new community with a different bishop, hoping he'd turn a blind eye to your situation. But since you've come to see me, it must not have worked out that way."

This woman was *schmaert*. *Ja*, he'd hoped the move might solve his problem, particularly since Hickory Springs was known to be a good bit less strict than Carroway. But it hadn't.

"Jakob wrote to Charley," he explained. "Likely my *aent* and *onkel* pestered him to."

"No doubt." Susie had finished moving the hot jars out of the canner. She now began transferring a new batch of filled jars into the bubbling water. "What do you do for a living?"

Eli blinked, surprised by the abrupt change of subject. "Furniture-making, mostly. I ran my own business over in Carroway, but now I'm working for my *kossin* Vernon over at Flaud's Furniture."

"Sounds like a step down. Unless you weren't doing so

well with your own store." She glanced at him, a smile quirking up the corner of her mouth. "Sorry. It's my business to ask nosy questions, I'm afraid."

Eli sighed. He supposed a matchmaker had to check on such things, to make sure the woman would be well provided for. "I did all right. And if things work out well with Vernon, I'll likely buy a half interest in his store in a year or two."

"Still, you'll only own half a business instead of a whole one. And you've taken on all the other trouble that comes with moving. Finding a house, settling into a new church." She finished loading the canner and turned to face him. "Seems to me you've gone to a fair amount of trouble to avoid taking a wife, Eli. Tell me the truth. Would you even be here talking to me if your relatives and the bishops hadn't backed you into a corner?"

"*Nee*, of course not."

Susie's eyebrows went up—and Eli knew that, once again, he'd said exactly the wrong thing. But what else could he have said? It was the truth.

"Well, you're honest. I'll give you that. But since that's the case, I'm afraid I can't help you. The best you'll get from me today is a jar of these pear preserves, a warm welcome to the community and the promise of my prayers."

Eli frowned at her. "You don't understand—"

"Oh, I understand your problem perfectly, and I'm very sorry for it. But it's clear that you don't really want a wife, and that you resent being pushed to take one. I can't encourage any young woman to marry a man who feels like that. It takes two to make a happy marriage, and both of them must be ready and willing."

"I *am* willing."

"That's only half of it. When you're ready to marry—

when you feel your life's incomplete without a woman to love—then you come back and see me, and we'll talk again."

He'd never be ready, so that was a problem. "What about the bishop?"

"You'll just have to hope for the best. I've known Charley Coblentz for years. He's a kind-hearted fellow who's been known to overlook things here and there. Once he gets to know you and your niece better, he might be willing to forget the whole thing." She sighed as she started to peel another pear. "Then again, he might not. Once Charley's spoken on a matter, he expects his congregation to do as he's told them. So I'm afraid this could go either way." She offered a sympathetic smile.

Eli didn't smile back. He didn't need this woman's sympathy. He needed her help. But clearly, he wasn't going to get it.

"There's only one way this can go," he assured her grimly. "I'm going to see to it."

He meant that. Leah was staying right where she belonged—with him, bishop or no bishop. If this matchmaker wasn't willing to help him, he'd find another way.

"*Denki* for your time," he said politely. Then he clapped his hat on his head and turned toward the door.

He needed to go off by himself where he could think clearly. Then he'd figure out what he could do to keep Leah with him. And whatever it was, he'd do it.

He had no choice.

Chapter Two

Out in the yard, Trudy cast an agonized look at Susie's back door—which remained stubbornly closed. How long had it been since the stranger had vanished into the house? It seemed like forever. She wondered what they were talking about. Or, more importantly, who.

Oh, she hoped they were talking about her.

"Look, Trudy!" Leah burrowed out of the tree, a pear clutched in her hand.

"That's a pretty one!"

Beaming, the little girl put the fruit in the washbasin. "There are lots," she said shyly. "I'll go get more!"

"*Wunderbaar*! I don't know what I'd have done if you hadn't come along to help me today!"

Leah gave a happy skip before disappearing under the limbs of the tree, bowed almost to the ground by the weight of the fruit.

The pear tree should have been pruned this past winter. Susie had trimmed the limbs she could reach as best she could, but some branches had been beyond her. The men of the community had planned on finishing the job. They always looked after Susie and other widows in town, seeing to whatever chores they couldn't manage.

But it had been a difficult winter with lots of unpleasant weather, and on the few decent days, the men's own work had to be seen to first. Somehow, Susie's pear tree had slipped through the season untrimmed.

Jeremiah Weaver had taken a long look at the tree the last time he and his wife, Anna, had stopped by for a visit. No doubt he'd see to the job himself sometime after cold weather set in. The farmer credited Susie with his recent happy marriage, and he made it his business to see that the matchmaker never went without.

Well, Jeremiah could tend to the pear tree this winter. But maybe, Trudy thought hopefully, just maybe, another grateful husband would be taking a turn next year.

Trudy cast another anxious look at the back door. A few minutes ago, she'd felt so hopeless, and now, this very minute, Susie was probably setting up a courtship. Not with some elderly widower, either, but with a nice-looking man not much older than she was herself—one who'd shown up at exactly the right time, just like a hero in one of those romance books.

It couldn't have been more perfect.

"Here!" Leah emerged from the leaves, holding another pear aloft. "This one was nicest, but there was another one, almost as pretty. I can get that one, too."

"You're doing a very *gut* job!" Trudy smiled as the little girl burrowed into the sagging branches. Leah seemed like a sweet girl. She was certainly eager to please, and she didn't shirk at helping. If Eli was raising his niece all on his own, he was doing a fine job of it. That spoke well of him.

She'd seen a few telltale signs that the girl didn't have a mother—but only a few. Her hair could have been better pinned up, and the hem on her dress needed to be let down about an inch. Details a man might not notice, but a woman would.

A *mamm* would.

The butterflies in her stomach fluttered. Depending on how the conversation in Susie's kitchen was going, she, Trudy Schwartz, might soon not only be someone's wife, but someone's *mamm*.

A dream come true, for certain sure.

The bang of the screen door made her heart catch in her throat. Eli was finally coming down the steps. She turned away, pretending to be focused on picking pears. Would he speak to her now? Ask if she was interested in going for a buggy ride to get ice cream? Or maybe invite her to take a walk so they could get better acquainted?

He cleared his throat, and the butterflies in her stomach fluttered harder.

"Trudy?"

"Ja?" She spoke lightly—as if her whole future didn't hang on this conversation.

"Where's Leah?"

Startled, she glanced over her shoulder. Eli held a jar of Susie's pears in one hand, and he didn't look bashful or hopeful at all.

He looked annoyed.

"In here, *onkel*!" Leah's voice came through the leaves. "I'm finding lots of *gut* pears for Trudy."

"Best hurry up." Eli sounded tired, but he spoke kindly. "We need to get on our way." He nodded curtly at Trudy. *"Denki* for watching her."

"It was no trouble. She's been a good helper." A few excruciating seconds ticked by as Trudy waited hopefully, but Eli said nothing further.

Finally she couldn't resist asking. "Did your talk with Susie go well?"

"Not really. Are there any other matchmakers around here that you know of?"

For a second, Trudy was so astonished that she couldn't answer.

"Nee," she managed finally. "Susie's the only one."

Leah rustled back out of the tree, a pear in each hand. She held them up triumphantly. "Two *gut* ones! See, Trudy?"

"That's—that's lovely." It was ridiculous how hard she found it to speak right now. Her disappointment had congealed into a lump in her throat. "Why don't you take those two with you? For you and your *onkel* to have with your supper?"

"Denki," Eli said. He nodded at the little girl. "What do we say, Leah?"

"Denki, Trudy. It was fun helping you!" She turned to her uncle. "I wish our new house had a pear tree."

"Maybe we'll plant one." He put one hand on Leah's shoulder, steering her gently toward the buggy.

Trudy stooped to pick up the tub of pears. It was only half full, but she didn't care. She was going inside to talk to Susie. She had to know what on earth had happened in that kitchen.

"Trudy?"

She turned at the sound of her name. Eli was standing beside his horse, looking in her direction. *"Ja?"*

"Did Susie say you worked as a nanny?"

"That's right. I work for an *Englisch* family in town."

"Are there any other women around here who do that sort of work? I'll need someone to look after Leah while I'm at my job."

She could barely think of her own name right now, much less anyone else's. "I'll... I'll have to think it over."

"I'm working at my cousin's store. Flaud's Furniture. You

know it?" When she nodded, he went on. "If you think of somebody, send her there."

"I will."

Without another word, he turned away and returned to the business of getting Leah settled in the buggy. Trudy stood in the yard, the basin of pears clutched against her chest, noting how gentle he was with the child, how he smiled at her and chucked her under the chin playfully, even though clearly he wasn't in a good mood.

The minute Eli's buggy had rolled out onto the road, she set her mouth in a tight line and mounted the back steps. She wanted answers.

She didn't get them.

"What was said stays between me and him," Susie repeated calmly.

"But why'd you send him away so quick? What's wrong with him?"

"Nothing. I think he and his niece will be fine additions to our community."

Trudy had never struck another human being in her life, but at the moment she felt she could cheerfully wring Susie's neck. "Then why didn't you at least suggest we talk to each other?"

"Eli's not ready to get married."

That didn't make any sense at all. "But he came here looking for a matchmaker, Susie!"

"You can't always go by what a person says. It's what's in the heart that counts, and Eli's not ready. Until he is, I can't help him, just like I couldn't can these pears until they were ripe." Susie stopped peeling her pear and gave Trudy a sympathetic look. "I know you're discouraged, but you're just going to have to trust me. Now, if you'd like a break from picking the pears, you can help me peel them."

Susie's tone made it clear their conversation was over. Trudy reluctantly dropped the subject, but the following afternoon when she walked the short distance over to the Johnsons' house to look after six-year-old Hayleigh, the disappointment was still weighing on her mind.

Why was Susie so convinced that Eli wasn't ready to get married? The man had come looking for a wife, after all. And Trudy was certainly looking for a husband. How much more ready could they be?

Maybe that offhand remark Susie had made—the one about Trudy possibly being a Good Apple Girl—had something to do with it. Was that why she wasn't making much effort to match Trudy up? Because after living together these few months, she'd decided Trudy was meant to be single?

Trudy's heart sank. If the town matchmaker believed that…maybe it was true.

"Gott," she whispered. "If it's Your will that I stay single all my life, please help me to be content and joyful alone. But," she added with a sigh, "I sure wish just one fellow had wanted to court me. Just one, even if it hadn't ended in a marriage. At least I'd have something sweet to remember."

She sighed and straightened her shoulders, pushing the gloom out of her mind as she walked up the short sidewalk to the Johnsons' large brick home. She'd been Hayleigh's nanny since the little girl was two years old, and she deserved Trudy's full attention.

Carlie Johnson met her at the door in her workout clothes, hair pulled back in a ponytail. That wasn't unusual. But today Mrs. Johnson looked embarrassed, and Hayleigh, who usually greeted Trudy with squeals and hugs, was nowhere in sight.

"I'm so sorry, Trudy. We won't be needing you this afternoon, after all. Hayleigh decided she wanted to take both ballet and tap." The woman hesitated, looking unhappy. "Those classes fill up her afternoons, so..."

It took Trudy a minute to understand what Mrs. Johnson was trying to tell her. Her part-time job had just evaporated.

"Oh!" Trudy was taken aback. This wasn't good news. Her income had been scanty enough already since the Johnsons had stopped needing her full-time.

"We should have let you know sooner, but we're so busy these days. I didn't even think about it until this morning, and since you don't have a phone, it's hard to get in touch with you at the last minute. I feel terrible. You know we all love you, and we hope you'll still be willing to babysit for us from time to time. Do you think you can pick up more work at that little store to make up the difference?"

Trudy occasionally helped out at the Farmhouse Pantry, a small grocery store run by Anna Weaver. Maybe Anna could use her more often.

However, a much more interesting idea was taking shape in her mind—and the more she thought about her new plan, the better she liked it.

Susie probably wouldn't approve, but Trudy didn't care. Before she accepted a future as a Good Apple Girl, she wanted to have another talk with Hickory Springs' newest bachelor.

"Isn't that swing ready for painting yet?" Eli's cousin Vernon leaned his head into the workshop from the doorway leading into the furniture showroom. "We've still got that order of chairs to get through."

Eli ran a finger down the swing's slatted oak back before he answered. "It needs a little more sanding."

Vernon made an exasperated noise. "It's a porch swing, Eli. It doesn't have to be perfect."

It did if Eli made it. But Vernon wouldn't understand so Eli only shrugged. "It won't take much longer."

The other man sighed and disappeared into the store to wait on customers.

Eli was glad to see him go. He liked Vernon, and he appreciated the opportunity his *kossin* had given him to come here and work in his store. The workshop was well-equipped, and Eli enjoyed working alone back here, undisturbed by the folks shopping out front.

He'd always had a knack for woodworking, but he'd never been good at dealing with customers. Here Vernon handled that, which was a welcome relief. Plus, he'd rented Eli and Leah his late parents' *dawdi haus* at a generous family discount. All in all, his *kossin* had been a huge blessing during the move to Hickory Ridge.

Sometimes, though, Vernon could be a pest. He liked things done quick, while Eli preferred to take his time and be sure each piece was done exactly right. Now and then, Eli missed his old workshop back in Carroway. It had been much simpler than this one, just a large shed in his own backyard with a hand-painted sign stuck out front, but he'd liked that better than being in the middle of town. There'd been no one rushing him, but on the other hand, he'd had to deal with customers himself. He wasn't *gut* with people, so that part hadn't always gone so well. He preferred being left alone when he worked.

Well, except for Leah, he reminded himself, smoothing the golden wood with firm, gentle strokes. For the past couple of years, his niece had spent a lot of time out in the old woodshop with him. He'd built a little corral for her where she could play safely with her toys, and he could keep an eye on her.

That had worked fine when it was just the two of them,

but it was out of the question here. Eli missed having the child nearby. Vernon's wife was keeping Leah today, and neither he nor Leah were too happy about the arrangement. Jane Flaud was a busy, no-nonsense woman who had little patience with his niece's strange fears. The miserable look on Leah's small face when he'd driven away from the house had troubled him all the morning.

He'd need to find someone else soon. Someone more like that Trudy woman he'd met over at the matchmaker's house. Leah had really taken to her, and she was usually so cautious with strangers. He'd thought it over later, trying to figure out what it was about Trudy that had made such a difference.

He hadn't been able to put his finger on it. Trudy looked like a very ordinary woman. Medium-brown hair, pear-green eyes and a slim build. Not too young and not too pretty, although nice enough looking. The only thing remarkable about her, so far as he could tell, was that big smile. It added a sweet friendliness to her expression that he'd liked—and he hardly ever noticed women's smiles.

Leah had certainly liked her. She'd chattered half the way home about picking the pears and the "secret room" inside the tree that Trudy had told her about. It seemed a silly story to him, but it had made Leah happy, and that's what counted.

Leah was what counted.

She was the reason he'd made this move and all these unsettling changes. He'd figured so long as he got to keep her with him, any amount of trouble was well worth it. His plan hadn't worked out so well, thanks to Bishop Coblentz and that uncooperative matchmaker.

He still couldn't quite wrap his head around Susie's refusal to help him. Matchmakers made matches, didn't they? And he'd only told her the truth.

He didn't want to get married. Mary had been right—he wasn't cut out for it. He'd never understood people—especially women. Somehow he always either hurt their feelings or made them mad. He never meant to. But he did.

That didn't mean he didn't get lonesome sometimes. He did. There just hadn't been much he could do about it. Then Leah had come along.

The tiny girl had turned his life upside down. She'd also given him a reason to get up in the morning and made him happier than he'd ever expected to be.

She seemed pretty happy with him, too. More importantly, she depended on him, and if he had to get married to keep her safe, he would. He wouldn't be any prize as a husband, but he'd never be unkind, at least not on purpose. And he'd make it his business to see that no woman in his household went without anything she needed.

Of course, she'd have to tell him straight out what she wanted. He'd never been good at guessing. Folks cared about so many things that made no sense to him.

Not that it mattered now. He'd no idea how he'd find a woman to court without the matchmaker's help. And at church this coming Sunday, Bishop Coblentz was bound to ask how his meeting with Susie had gone. Eli was dreading that conversation.

"Eli!" Vernon shouted from the front. "Visitor coming back to see you!"

Eli looked up from his work and frowned. There was something odd in Vernon's tone. Not irritation or disapproval, which Eli could have understood since this visitor was interrupting a busy workday.

Nee, his *kossin* sounded…amused.

"All right." Eli stopped sanding and waited to see who'd come to see him.

When Trudy appeared in the doorway, looking nervous—and determined—Eli stared at her. What on earth was she doing here?

"Hello, Eli. I'm sorry to disturb you at your work, but you asked if I knew of anyone who'd be a good nanny for Leah."

"I did, *ja*." He set down his sandpaper and wiped his dusty hands quickly on his trousers. "So you have some names for me?"

"Only one." A babble of customer's voices sounded behind her, followed by Vernon's friendly salesman chuckle. Trudy glanced over her shoulder, clearly uncomfortable.

She wasn't the only one. He didn't know who Trudy would suggest, and he was going to have some questions. He didn't want to put Leah through half a dozen babysitters before they found the right one.

Maybe if he explained his worries about Leah, Trudy could help him decide if this woman she knew would be a good fit. But conversation didn't come easily to him, and he'd rather not talk where his *kossin* might overhear. He thought fast.

"Can you walk across to the park with me so we can talk?"

"*Ja*, sure."

"It's not far—" He stopped short. He'd expected to have to talk her into it. In his experience, women wanted to hear a lot of explanations and reasons before they agreed to something. But Trudy had agreed right away.

"All right, then." He led the way back through the furniture store where Vernon was busy talking some *Englisch* customers into buying a large oval table that came with eight chairs. They didn't have it in stock, so if he succeeded, Eli's workload would triple. Since his *kossin* usually did succeed, Eli hoped Trudy's suggestion for a nanny was a good one.

"I'll be back in a few minutes, Vernon."

A funny change came over his *kossin*'s face. He looked as if he wanted to say something—and didn't want to—all at the same time. He stayed silent for a full five seconds scratching his beard—a long time for Vernon, who was, in Eli's opinion, overfond of talking.

Finally, the other man shrugged, a twinkle in his eye. "Don't be long."

Eli didn't bother to reply. He never took long on his breaks, and, anyway, this conversation was about Leah, so he wouldn't rush it. Vernon would simply have to wait.

He and Trudy walked outside into the warm fall afternoon and crossed the street, heading for the small park. He'd taken Leah there a time or two since they'd moved to Hickory Springs. She liked the swings.

"Oh, my! Just look at those clouds!"

Startled out of his thoughts, Eli squinted up at the sky. What was the woman worried about? Plenty of clouds, *ja*, but they were all white and fluffy.

"I don't think it's going to rain. But if a shower pops up, there are shelters at the park."

She looked taken aback. "I'm not worried about rain. I just meant…the clouds look so pretty against the blue sky."

"Oh." He felt a little embarrassed that he'd mistaken her point, but he'd never understood why women liked to talk so much about things that really didn't matter. It made a difference if it rained. It didn't make much difference if the sky looked pretty or not.

But Leah was already much the same, chattering away about everything she saw. Pears and birds. Puddles and puppies. Likely when she grew up, she'd talk about how pretty clouds were, too, so he'd better learn how to talk back.

He cleared his throat. "*Ja*, they're real nice."

Trudy flashed an uncertain smile, but he must not have sounded too convincing because she didn't say anything else. They walked the rest of the way in silence, and he was thankful the park was so close by.

The place was never very crowded, and there were big oaks for shade and plenty of picnic tables and benches. Eli liked being around trees and grass. He thought better in places like that, so he figured the park would be a good place to talk. Maybe he wouldn't make such a hash of it here.

They found a bench beneath a big tree and sat, leaving a polite gap between them.

"So, tell me about this nanny you know. She's a *gut* one?"

Trudy took a long time to answer what he'd thought was a very simple question. "I think so."

"Not a *youngie*, I hope. Leah needs somebody with experience."

"Why?" Trudy suddenly seemed to forget about being *naerfich* and studied him with a sharp interest. "She's a very well-behaved child. She was certainly no trouble when I watched her."

His heart warmed at the praise for his niece, but he had to be honest. "She liked you, right off. That doesn't happen too often."

"And if she doesn't like someone, she'll misbehave?"

Eli hesitated. He never felt comfortable sharing details about his troubled family, so he always tried to explain as little as possible. "*Nee*, it's not that. She just cries and gets upset anytime something is new or difficult. Leah had a hard start in life, and it's made her more fearful than other children. She needs someone who can understand that and be patient with her."

"I see." Trudy appeared to think this over. "How long has she been with you?"

"I've taken care of her since she was two years old. The trouble happened before that." He paused, wondering how much he should tell Trudy about Leah's past.

Everyone in Carroway had known Leah's story—or as much of it as Eli knew himself. Here, it was different. Charley knew, of course, and Vernon and Jane because they were family. And he'd explained about Abby to Susie Raber, figuring it only fair that the matchmaker should know, too.

As it turned out, that hadn't mattered, and now he decided that nobody in Hickory Springs needed to know any more than what he'd told Leah herself.

"Leah's *mamm*—my sister, Abby—has some troubles that mean she can't take care of a little one. She tried at first, but things got pretty bad, and Leah suffered for it. Abby loves Leah, so she brought her to me, and now I look after her, best I can." So far, Leah seemed content with that explanation, and he figured other people could be content with it, too. "I thought she probably wouldn't remember anything about the hard time because she was so little, but—"

"Little children remember more than we think," Trudy said softly. "Maybe not so's they can explain it. But they remember in their feelings, and those memories come out in funny ways sometimes."

Eli looked at the woman sitting beside him with some surprise and a new respect. That made sense. It was the best explanation he'd ever heard—far more simple and true-sounding than all the gobbledygook he'd heard from that *Englisch* doctor.

He nodded. "That's so. I need a woman who'll understand that and not be harsh when Leah gets upset over silly things. Do you think this nanny you know would be a good fit?"

A firm nod. "*Ja*. I do."

Eli felt a wave of relief. Maybe this was going to work out.

"*Gut*. Leah's four now, so I've a couple of years before she starts school. I'll need somebody to watch her while I'm working, and I'm willing to pay well for the right person. So? Who do you have in mind?"

Trudy had been listening attentively, but at his question she flushed. "Well..." She clamped her hands together in her lap, straightened her shoulders and looked him in the eye. "Me."

Chapter Three

"You?" Eli blinked. "I thought you already had a job." She'd told him that, hadn't she? Back at the matchmaker's?

"I did, but the *Englisch* children I've been taking care of are in so many after-school activities, they don't need me now. I'm sure the Johnsons will be happy to give me a good reference if you want one."

"*Nee*, don't trouble them." He didn't trust *Englisch* thinking, not after seeing how that world had destroyed his sister. "You truly want this job?"

"I do. And I understand about Leah's troubles, and I'll be careful of her feelings. But," she went on, "I'll also be encouraging her to trust *Gott* and to work past her fears."

That was exactly what Eli hoped to do himself. He nodded cautiously.

"I'm available for the hours you'll need, and I've plenty of experience. And," she went on with a light laugh, "I'm not a *youngie*."

"*Nee*, you're certain sure not." Eli spoke absently, his mind already busy turning over this new idea. It wasn't until he glanced at Trudy's face that he realized he'd said the wrong thing.

He wasn't sure why it bothered her. After all, it was true. She wasn't a *youngie*, which in his mind was a definite advantage. Not that Plain girls weren't responsible and dependable—well, Abby hadn't been. But most were. However, a child with Leah's troubles needed somebody with experience. Trudy had plenty of that.

However, she didn't look so pleased at having that fact pointed out, so he tried to find some way to make amends.

"Besides, Leah already likes you." That was the biggest selling point as far as Eli was concerned, and the highest compliment he could pay her. "All right. Let's try it for a week and see how it goes. When can you start?"

Her face brightened. "Tomorrow. You can drop her by Susie's house in the morning on your way to work, if that suits."

"It'll suit well enough." Leah would be uneasy, spending the day in a new place, but that couldn't be helped. And at least she'd been to Susie's before and had a nice time.

They talked briefly about hours and salary. Once again, Trudy was more agreeable than he'd expected, and it didn't take long to get the details figured out.

When everything was settled, Eli stood. "I'd better be getting back to work now."

Trudy nodded and got to her feet. She looked pleased, and there was a pretty flush along her cheeks—probably because he'd offered a very nice salary, the top end of what he could afford. If Leah liked this arrangement as well as he figured she would, he wanted Trudy to be content with their deal.

"I guess I'll see you tomorrow, then," she said pleasantly.

"*Ja.* Tomorrow."

They parted company at the sidewalk, him turning toward the furniture store and her walking over to a shady spot where she'd left her horse and buggy. He stopped and watched to make sure she had no trouble, but she unhitched with quick, efficient movements, and navigated the buggy safely onto the road with no hesitation.

He liked that. He admired how she'd talked with him about their arrangement, too. Nice and clear and quick. *Ja*, he thought with some relief. This was a smart woman. Likely she'd take care of Leah well.

After she'd driven away, Eli walked back to the furniture store feeling more optimistic than he had all week. It would be fun, telling Leah that Trudy would be her nanny now. She'd be so excited that he'd probably have a hard time getting her to sleep tonight.

He'd had some trouble with bedtimes since the move, but at least this was a change she'd be happy about. He didn't mind losing any amount of sleep over that.

As he pulled open the door to the furniture store, he paused to glance up at the sky.

Trudy was right. Those clouds were kind of pretty.

Inside the showroom, Vernon stood alone at the counter, scribbling on a pad. He looked pleased with himself, so no doubt the *Englisch* customers had bought the table. He smirked as Eli walked in.

"Did you two have a nice talk?"

Eli halted, confused. Why was this funny? "Nice enough, I guess. I've hired her to be Leah's nanny."

"You hired Trudy Schwartz?" Vernon slapped the counter and guffawed.

Eli studied his *kossin* with alarm. "You'd best explain to me what's going on. Is Trudy not to be trusted?"

"With little ones? *Ja*, sure she can be trusted." Another snort of laughter. "But with a bachelor? Not if he wants to stay one. Everybody knows Trudy's looking for a husband. She must have her eye on you now."

Eli's frown deepened. His *kossin*'s amusement seemed

unkind—and untrue. "This was business. She needed a job, and I'd told her I wanted someone to look after Leah. That's the whole of it."

"That so?" Vernon raised an eyebrow. "I thought she already had a job, working for some *Englisch* family."

Eli shrugged. "That situation changed."

"Probably about the time she heard you were looking for a nanny, ain't so?" When Eli didn't answer, Vernon chuckled again. "I'd heard Trudy moved in with our local matchmaker, and likely Susie's behind this. That woman will stop at nothing to make a match. *Ach*, stop glaring at me. I'm only funning. Nothing wrong with it. High time you got married, anyway."

Eli struggled to control his temper. Vernon was irritating him with all this gossipy talk—especially since none of it was true. Susie had made herself very clear yesterday. She'd never have nudged Trudy or any other woman in his direction.

Of course, Vernon had no way of knowing that—and Eli wasn't about to tell him. He'd never hear the end of it if his *kossin* found out he'd gone to see the town matchmaker—and been turned down flat.

"I'm hiring Trudy to look after Leah, and that's all I'm doing. Now, I'm getting back to work on that swing." He headed across the store toward the workshop. "Going by that silly grin on your face, you've added a table and chairs to my work list."

"That's so," Vernon said smugly. "Good thing, seeing as how I'll likely be buying somebody a wedding present before long."

Eli didn't bother to reply, but as he picked up his sander, a troubling thought occurred to him. Since Trudy was living with the matchmaker—and assuming she was as anxious to get married as Vernon said—Eli was surprised Susie hadn't at least mentioned her when Eli showed up at her home. But she hadn't. She hadn't seemed interested in helping Eli at all.

He'd only told her the truth. He didn't like being herded into a courtship, and he wasn't interested in getting married. Up until now, that hadn't been much of a problem, since no girl had shown any interest in marrying him.

Not that he blamed them. He'd never been able to figure women out, not even his sister, Abby. They cared so much about things that just didn't make any sense to him. Like whether you remembered every detail of the day you'd met or noticed that they'd added a different spice to a soup, or that they had a new dress on.

They cried easily, too, over things a man couldn't fix for them, like a stillborn calf or a frost-nipped flower garden. When you tried to help by pointing out that there'd be other calves born sooner or later, and that flowers weren't much good for anything, not like vegetables, it only made them cry harder.

Maybe that was really why Susie hadn't offered to arrange a courtship with Trudy—maybe somehow she'd guessed how hopeless he was with women. A matchmaker was probably extra smart about such things.

Of course, there could be a very different reason. Could be she'd already found Trudy a match.

The more he thought about that idea, the more sense it made. He didn't know why Trudy wasn't already married, but he certainly saw nothing wrong with her. She was nice-looking, neat and pleasant. She got to her point quickly, and she seemed to know her own mind better than most. And she sure had a winning way with children.

He didn't know anything about matchmaking, but as far as he could tell, matching up Trudy Schwartz ought to have been a quick job. Engagements were generally kept secret until the upcoming wedding was announced at church, so could be Vernon just didn't know about Trudy's yet.

Eli frowned. That might be a problem. After Trudy married, she wouldn't be likely to keep on working as a nanny. Leah would be upset—and that doctor with the big words had warned Eli about that. Changing caregivers was hard on little ones, he'd said. Leah had already suffered through one big change, and that, the doctor had said, could be part of the reason why she had so many fears.

If Trudy was planning on getting married soon, he'd be better off finding another nanny. Which meant he'd have to ask Trudy right out if there was a wedding in her future—and he'd really rather not. First off, that wasn't something polite people asked. Besides, knowing him, he'd ask in just the wrong way—he usually did. Still, there was no way around it. He needed to know Trudy's plans before Leah got too attached.

Eli shook his head in frustration. He'd thought he had this problem well settled, and now he had another wrinkle to deal with.

He should've seen this coming. Things never worked out for Eli—not when a woman was involved. And yet the bishops—two of them—thought he ought to get married!

Eli huffed out a weary sigh and bent his head back over his sanding.

Late the following afternoon, Trudy and Leah stood together at Susie's kitchen table where they'd assembled all the ingredients for a big batch of chocolate chip cookies. Trudy smiled encouragingly at the little girl and held out a smooth brown egg.

"You can do it," she insisted gently. "Just crack the egg on the edge of the bowl."

Leah shook her head. "I can't."

Trudy kept her smile in place. This had been happening all day long. Any time she was confronted with something new, Leah balked.

"Just because you've never done something before, that doesn't mean you can't. Don't worry about making a mess. We'll just clean it up. Trust me, I've made plenty of messes in my time."

That was true—and according to Susie this new job might be Trudy's biggest mess so far. When Trudy had broken the news last night, the matchmaker had listened, her lips pressed into a tight unhappy line.

"I wish you'd talked to me about this first, Trudy."

"Will it be a problem? Me keeping Leah here during the workday?" She'd worried about that. This was Susie's home, after all, and if she objected to this arrangement...

"I'm not bothered about that. I'm worried you're setting yourself up to get hurt. There are some things you just can't rush, Trudy, not if you want them to turn out well. Every baker knows that—and every matchmaker, too." The older woman had sighed. "Well, what's done is done. Maybe this will turn out better than I expect."

She didn't sound hopeful, but then again, Trudy hadn't expected that Susie would like this idea. And Trudy wasn't rushing anything. She was just...nudging things along a little. Which she wouldn't have had to do in the first place if Susie hadn't been such a slowpoke.

With a sigh, Trudy pulled her mind back to the task at hand. Making cookies was one of her favorite icebreaker activities with a new child. She'd found it a smart way to figure out certain things about children—whether they could follow directions well, whether they were careless or cautious, how they reacted to frustration. Those were handy things to know about a child she was responsible for.

Right now, all she was learning about Leah was that the child was scared to crack an egg. The little girl stood frozen on her step stool, staring at the egg in Trudy's hand as if it was a snake.

Moving slowly, Trudy set the egg next to the mixing bowl in front of Leah and picked up the second one.

"Your *onkel* will be here to pick you up soon. Does he like chocolate chip cookies?"

"Ja," whispered Leah, frowning at the egg. "He likes them lots."

"We'd better get these in the oven, then. Tell you what. I'll crack one egg, and you crack the other one. I'll go first." She cracked the egg briskly into the bowl, then smiled at Leah. "Now it's your turn."

Leah reluctantly picked up the egg, her little forehead puckered. What Eli had said in the park was certainly proving true. The child was far too *naerfich* over the simple task, and she was clearly terrified of making a mistake.

But her love for her *onkel* won the day. Leah took a breath and cracked the egg against the side of the bowl. Most of the egg slid obediently into the flour mixture, with only a little of the white oozing down the outside of the bowl. Leah shot her a worried look, but Trudy whisked the goo away quickly with a paper towel.

"Very *gut*," she said, handing the child a big spoon.

Leah looked up at Trudy, her eyes wide.

"I did it. I cracked it, and it went right in the bowl. Mostly."

"You sure did! Now we'll get everything mixed up, and

the cookies should be ready by the time your *onkel* gets here. Won't that be a nice surprise for him?"

The prospect of pleasing Eli and her success with the egg seemed to do the trick. Leah stirred and scooped the batter with a clumsy enthusiasm that warmed Trudy's heart, and the rest of the cookie-making lesson went smoothly. The last tray of treats was just coming out of the oven when Eli's buggy rolled into the drive.

Leah had been tasked with moving the cooled cookies into a tin for safekeeping. She immediately abandoned that job and hopped down from the chair, beaming.

"He's here!" Before Trudy could speak, the little girl scampered out the door and ran across the yard.

Trudy started to call her back, then changed her mind. Setting the sheet of hot cookies on the stove, she tiptoed to peek out the kitchen window. The little girl reached the buggy just as Eli was getting out. The man swung his niece up into his arms, gave her a hug and then listened solemnly as she chattered to him.

Safely hidden behind the blue side curtain, Trudy watched Eli carry Leah toward the house, her heart swelling with a familiar longing. She'd wished all her life for something just like this—a little house, a *mann* and a child of her own. But this—helping out in someone else's home, caring for someone else's child—was the closest she'd gotten.

So far, anyway.

When Eli came into the kitchen, he looked uneasy. No doubt he was wondering how their first day had gone.

"Leah and I had a very nice time," Trudy assured him.

"We made cookies!" Leah announced. "Chocolate chip. Your favorite! And we get to take some home with us!"

"That's nice." Eli set his niece down and cleared his throat awkwardly. "Trudy, can we talk for a minute?"

Trudy had picked up the mixing bowl, planning to carry it to the sink to wash, but at his tone, she paused and frowned. He didn't sound pleased, and that didn't make sense. Leah was happy, and their day together had gone perfectly fine, with no unexpected problems at all. Setting the bowl back on the table, Trudy turned to face him.

"Of course. What about?"

Eli glanced at Leah. The little girl had climbed back up on her step stool, intent on moving the rest of the cookies to the tin. "Could we…uh…step outside?"

Trudy's frown deepened. "*Ja*, sure. Leah, we'll be right back."

She wasn't sure how the child would react. Throughout the day, Leah had stayed right under Trudy's skirts. But now that Eli was here, the little girl seemed more relaxed, and she nodded happily.

"I'll put the rest of the cookies up," she announced importantly.

"*Denki*. That will be a big help," Trudy said with a smile. Then, her heart in her throat, she followed Eli out onto Susie's back stoop.

The September afternoon was lovely, washed in a golden light, with a warm breeze wafting the scent of the remaining pears toward the house. There was no chill in the air yet, but something about the slant of the light hinted that autumn would set in soon. The last of summer was quickly fading away, Trudy realized sadly.

Eli moved as far from her as he could get on the small stoop, leaning against the railing. He cleared his throat, but he didn't seem to know how to get started.

After a few awkward seconds, Trudy tried a nudge. "If you're worried about Leah, she really seemed to have a *gut* day. It's true what you said about her being uneasy with changes, but all things considered, I think we got along real well."

"*Nee*, it's not that." He sounded uncomfortable. "I could tell the minute she ran outside that she'd had a happy day. That's part of the problem."

"I don't understand. Has something happened that I don't know about?"

"I heard something about you in town that makes me think you won't be keeping this job very long."

Trudy's knees went wobbly, and she groped behind herself to find the handrail to lean on. Oh, she didn't like how this conversation was going. "Something about me?" She tried to imagine what that might be, but she couldn't come up with anything terrible.

Eli's cheeks went ruddy, and a muscle twitched in his jaw, but he looked back at her, a glint of desperate determination in his eyes. "My *kossin* Vernon told me you're looking for a husband. Which makes sense, I guess, seeing as how you're living over at the matchmaker's house."

"Oh!" Trudy's face burned so hot she was sure it was the color of a beet, but as humiliated as she felt, she couldn't deny it.

When women moved into Susie's spare room, everybody in Hickory Springs knew what they were hoping for, even if they were too tactful to say so. She knew how the men joked when Susie had a new tenant under her roof, warning all the bachelors to duck for cover when they saw the matchmaker coming down the street.

Unless, of course, they happened to be interested in the woman. Which, clearly, Eli wasn't.

She'd imagined so many ways this first day might play out, sweet ways, hopeful ways, and *ja*, a few disappointing ways. But she'd not imagined anything so embarrassing as this. Susie had—as usual—been exactly right. Trudy had rushed things and caused a mess. To her horror, she felt humiliated tears prickling in her eyes.

She sniffled, and Eli leaned forward to get a better look at her face. His uneasiness shifted to horror so fast that—under different circumstances—it might have been funny.

"I've gone and made you cry! *Ach*," he muttered, as if to himself. "I've made a muck of things like I always do. I didn't mean to shame you. I went there myself, didn't I? To the matchmaker's? Not that it did me any good."

He sounded so annoyed that Trudy blinked at him with baffled surprise. He met her eyes briefly, then returned his gaze to his boots.

"If it wasn't for Leah… But you've spent a day with her now, and no doubt you've seen for yourself how *naerfich* she is, how hard new things can be for her. So I had to ask you. I didn't have a choice."

Trudy was so thoroughly confused that she forgot to be embarrassed. "Ask me what? If it's true what your *kossin* told you? That I'm looking for a husband?"

"*Nee*. Not that." He looked up and studied her, his brow furrowed. "I'm asking if you've already found one."

Chapter Four

Trudy sucked in a sharp breath of air. At long last, it had finally happened. A man was asking if she was available for courting.

She'd imagined this moment a thousand times, pulling sweet bits from the books she'd read, since she didn't have any real-life experiences to go by. In her mind, the fellow asking had looked hopeful or embarrassed or maybe endearingly *naerfich*.

Eli, on the other hand, only looked worried and uncomfortable. Maybe even a little irritated. In fact, his expression right now reminded her of her *daed*'s face on the last visiting Sunday, just after he'd discovered a leak under the kitchen sink.

That wasn't particularly flattering.

"So?" Eli prodded after a few seconds. "It's a simple question. Are you planning to marry somebody or not?"

Trudy blinked. Well, he was right. The question was simple enough.

"*Nee*, I'm not planning to marry anybody." She held her breath, waiting to see what he'd say next.

"Are you sure?"

Trudy's breath sputtered out in surprised indignation.

"Of course, I'm sure! I'd know, wouldn't I? If I was planning on getting married?"

"I suppose you would, *ja*." He still didn't sound entirely convinced. "Well, then that matchmaker woman can't be so *gut* at her job as the bishop thinks," he muttered.

"Susie has a real knack for making matches," Trudy protested loyally. "She's just…careful. It's a big responsibility, matchmaking."

"How long has she kept you waiting?"

Trudy felt her cheeks growing hot. This was getting very personal, but given the circumstances, she supposed he had the right to ask. "I moved in with Susie at the beginning of the summer, so three months or so."

"Three months." Eli shook his head. "That makes no sense to me. Unless—" He shot her a sharp, searching look. "Do you even want to get married? Did somebody make you work with the matchmaker? Like a parent or…say… the bishop, maybe?"

"Nobody made me." Hope stirred in her heart. *That makes no sense*, he'd said. That was a compliment—wasn't it? "It was my own idea, moving in with Susie."

"And you're telling me she's not come up with any fellow for you yet? Why not?"

Trudy hesitated. She certain sure wasn't going to share Susie's remark that Trudy might turn out to be a Good Apple Girl. That was not an idea she wanted to put in Eli's head.

"There aren't so many bachelors in Hickory Springs just now. I mean, not…" she stammered "…not ones close to my age."

"*Ja*, you're older than most Plain girls when they marry," Eli agreed matter-of-factly, rubbing his chin. "So, there's that, I suppose. But still, I don't see the trouble. You seem plenty healthy and *schmaert*."

Healthy and *schmaert*? The hopeful warmth blooming in Trudy's heart died like a campfire dashed with water. She might not have any first-hand courtship experience, but she'd read dozens of romances. And never once in any of them could she recall a fellow admiring a woman for being healthy and *schmaert*.

For pity's sake, Eli sounded like he was buying a horse.

She opened her mouth to tell him so, then stopped short. *Mamm* and Susie both had cautioned her about letting her *Englisch* romance books give her silly expectations about love and marriage. Most Plain men, they'd assured her, weren't like the men in those books. They tended to be much more practical.

And she shouldn't lose sight of the fact that an unmarried fellow was talking about courtship with her—with *her*, a woman no man had ever shown any serious interest in before. That was nothing to sneeze at.

Before she could decide how best to answer him, Eli frowned.

"Is it possible that this matchmaker, this Susie, has a courtship set up for you and just hasn't told you about it yet?"

Well, at least she knew the answer to that. "*Nee*. I'm sure she doesn't."

"Ah." He studied her for another moment, then nodded as if satisfied. "Well, that's a puzzlement, but it's *gut* news for me and Leah." He gave a rueful shrug. "I'm sorry," he added, "for asking so many nosy questions. But Susie wasn't too inclined to be helpful to me, so I didn't figure there was any use in my asking her. And I needed to know how things stood before I went any further with this. You understand, *ja*?"

"I...suppose I do. Of course, you'd...you'd need to know."

"Denki," he offered gruffly. "For not being mad. I know I'm clumsy with my words sometimes." He took a deep breath and nodded. "I don't mind telling you, this is a big relief. I'm real glad things can move forward. Leah likes you an awful lot."

He craned his neck so he could look through the kitchen window. Trudy followed his gaze. Leah was busy transferring the last of the cookies from the sheet into the little tin, smiling as she did. She looked the picture of contentment, and Trudy felt her own lips curving upward.

"I'm glad to hear it. I like her, too."

She couldn't help noticing that he'd only talked about how much Leah liked her. He'd not mentioned anything about liking her himself. Not yet, anyway.

He cleared his throat, and her heart flip-flopped hopefully.

"It looks like Leah's about done with those cookies, so I guess we'll be off home now." He moved toward the door, leaving Trudy staring after him in surprise.

"That's it? We're through talking?"

Eli stopped short, one hand on the doorknob. He turned to look at her, his brow furrowed. "*Ja,* I think so. For now, anyways. Unless there's something else you need to tell me?"

Trudy's mouth was dry, and her heart was beating too fast. "Nothing else I need to tell you, *nee.* But maybe there's something *you* need to tell *me.*"

He looked genuinely puzzled. "What's that?"

She swallowed, but she'd gone too far to turn back now. "You said *Leah* likes me."

"Right."

Trudy waited, but he only looked at her.

Finally, exasperated, she put her hands on her hips. "Well,

I'd hope to hear *you* like me, too! At least, you know...a little."

"Oh! Sorry." He smiled at her, just a brief apologetic flash of a smile, but it changed his face so much her breath caught in her throat. "Like I said, I'm clumsy with my words. *Ja*, Trudy, sure. I like you real well. I guess I should have said as much, although I can't see why I'd need to spell it out. If I didn't like you, we'd not be having this conversation at all."

With that, he pulled open the door and went inside to collect Leah. Trudy stood alone on the little stoop, pressing one hand over her pounding heart and struggling to gather her wits.

Well, that long-awaited moment sure hadn't gone the way she'd expected—and if she were honest, not quite the way she'd hoped. On the other hand, a man—and a youngish, nice-looking one at that—had just asked if she were available for courting and even said straight out that he liked her.

Maybe it had taken a little prodding, but still. He'd said it, and she'd seen in his face that he meant it. She wasn't about to quibble over the details.

Eli emerged from Susie's kitchen, leading Leah by the hand. The child carried the tin of cookies and was smiling from ear to ear.

"See you tomorrow!" the little girl chirped happily.

Trudy smiled back. "See you tomorrow! Both of you," she added, glancing up at Eli to include him in her smile.

But Eli wasn't looking at her. His eyes were on Susie's buggy, just turning into the drive. "We'd best get along home," he muttered. He swung Leah up in his arms and hurried to the buggy, giving Susie a polite nod.

Susie nodded back nicely enough, but when she glanced at Trudy, her eyes narrowed suspiciously. Trudy offered a quick wave and hurried back into the kitchen.

As she finished tidying up the kitchen, she tried to think about how to explain this new situation to Susie. She hadn't come up with much before Susie had finished the unhitching and appeared in the doorway to the kitchen.

"What," she asked as she untied her bonnet, "was that all about? Eli looked like a possum who'd been caught in the henhouse."

As Trudy stumbled through her explanation, Susie's kind face pinched into worried lines.

"Oh, dear." Still clutching her black bonnet, Susie sank into the kitchen chair. "You've begun a courtship with Eli Mast? I'm... I'm not entirely sure that's a good idea."

Not *entirely* sure. Trudy felt a whiff of relief. That wasn't so bad.

She straightened her spine and clenched her hands together. "Well, it's the best idea I could come up with. I don't want to be a Good Apple Girl, Susie. I want to get married."

Susie laughed—a short mirthless sound. "*Ja*, I know you do. Are you sure Eli does?"

"Surely he must. I know you think he's not ready, but why on earth would he ask me about courting if he wasn't seriously interested in getting married? Or even come here in the first place, looking for a matchmaker? Since you wouldn't help him, I suppose he figured he'd better ask me for himself."

"Did he tell you exactly why he came looking for a matchmaker?"

"*Nee*, he didn't."

"Did you ask?" When Trudy shook her head, Susie sighed. "You should ask more questions, Trudy. You really should."

"If you think I need to know, why don't you just tell me yourself?"

"I'm not a gossip, Trudy. When someone comes to me looking for help finding a match, I never share what they tell me with other folks." She darted a sharp glance up at Trudy's face. "But take my advice and ask Eli yourself."

She pushed herself to her feet and went to hang her bonnet on the peg by the door. Trudy watched her uneasily.

"That's all you're going to say?"

"*Ja.* For now." Susie straightened the bonnet with a stern tug. "But the next time I see him, I'm having another little talk with Eli Mast."

It was almost time for the Sunday service to start by the time Eli drove into the Yoder family farmyard. The men had already drifted out of the barn and were heading toward the house. People were sorting themselves out, preparing to file in, and he still had to unhitch and tie his horse to the fence with the others.

He wasn't sorry he'd missed the hang-around-and-talk time that always preceded the services, but it wasn't *gut* to be late. He should have gotten here earlier. He would have, but Leah was having a hard morning.

As he went rapidly through the familiar motions of getting the buggy and his horse situated, the little girl trailed closely behind him—so close that he almost stumbled over her a time or two. She might look as sweet as strawberry pie in her dark pink dress, but her forehead was puckered ominously, and her mouth was trembling. She was on the brink of another meltdown—her second so far today.

Leah hadn't wanted to come to church. She'd sobbed hysterically when it was time to leave with Vernon and his family, so Eli had told his *kossin* to go ahead. He'd pretended not to notice the look Jane had thrown his way, but of course, he'd known what it meant.

He and Leah couldn't skip church, not with the bishop already in the middle of their business. What would Bishop Coblentz think if Eli couldn't even get his niece to church on a Sunday? No doubt it would be yet another reason for the bishops to take her away, and he couldn't allow that.

By pulling out every trick he knew to calm her down, he'd finally managed to get her in the buggy. But she wasn't happy about being here.

"It's all right," he told her now, for the dozenth time. "Everything's new here for us right now, so it feels strange, but before long we'll know everybody just like we did back in Carroway."

Leah snuffled sadly. He knew this was difficult for her. Change always was. Living in a new church district, with new faces and new homes every other Sunday was a lot for Leah to cope with.

It wasn't easy for him, either. He felt uncomfortable even around most people he knew, let alone strangers. His was a strange situation among the Amish, a never-married man parenting a little child. People in his church group in Carroway had been familiar with his family troubles, so there'd been no odd glances. So far people had been kind here, but naturally there was some curiosity. Sooner or later, that would lead to questions he'd prefer to avoid.

He finished tying off the horse and took Leah's hand. "Come along now," he said gently.

To his relief, she accepted his hand and trudged along beside him, hanging her head. He sighed. He and Leah would both get used to Hickory Springs. They had no choice.

As they walked across the yard to the house, he tried to hurry, but Leah dragged her feet. He was just about to pick her up, when her fingers tightened around his.

"Look, Eli! There's Trudy!"

Sure enough, Trudy was on the porch, standing in a group of other single women. She waved at them, spoke briefly to her friends, and then started down the steps in their direction.

To Eli's surprise, Leah immediately let go of his hand and hurried over to meet Trudy. She tipped the little girl's chin up with a finger and then tapped her playfully on the nose.

And Leah—wonder of wonders—laughed. Just as if the whole awful morning had never happened. Surprised, Eli stopped walking and stared at the pair of them.

The early morning sunlight was filtering pleasantly through the leaves, just now turning golden. The colored light played over them softly, and when Trudy glanced over at him and smiled, Eli felt like a mule had kicked him right in his middle. His knees actually went weak.

Maybe it was just relief that Leah's mood had shifted so quickly. Maybe it was a trick of that golden light, making everything—and everyone—look a little prettier and sweeter. He wasn't sure.

What he did know was that he'd never felt so glad to see anybody, not in his whole life.

She waited where she was, holding Leah's hand in her own until he reached them.

"Gut mariye," she said. "It's nice to see you."

"You, too," he managed with some difficulty.

"Trudy comes to this church, too!" Leah's eyes were shining with happiness, and she was bouncing on her toes.

"I wasn't at the last meeting because I was helping a sick *aent*," Trudy explained. "I was wondering…maybe Leah would like to sit with me during services?"

Leah bounced up and down faster. *"Ja! Ja*, I would. May I? Please?"

"Sure," Eli murmured. "So long as you don't mind…" He

directed that to Trudy, giving her an out in case Leah had begged this favor before he'd gotten within earshot.

Trudy answered without hesitation. "I don't mind a bit, so long as you don't."

Eli frowned. Why on earth would he mind? Women at his former church had often looked after Leah during services, particularly when she was younger. Traditionally, children sat with the women, so they'd simply gathered her up with their own children, leaving him to sit alone with the men.

He'd appreciated that, especially at first when he'd needed all the help he could get. He'd certainly never objected—not until about six months ago, when Leah had started crying before church because she didn't want to sit next to her stern great *aent*.

After that, he'd kept Leah with him. That had raised some eyebrows, and if he'd stayed in Carroway much longer, likely his bishop would have spoken to him about it.

But, of course, he was fine with Leah sitting with Trudy. "*Nee*, I don't mind."

"All right, then!" Trudy's smile brightened, and the flush on her cheeks deepened. "I guess we'd best hurry. It's time to go in." She led Leah across the yard and up on the porch where she and the child were welcomed into the group of single women lining up for entry. He noticed that Trudy was close to the front of that line, meaning she was one of the older *maidels*.

Most women were married and had two or three *kinder* by the time they were Trudy's age. Not that he knew exactly how old she was.

He found his own place in the line of single men. He was near the front of that line himself, of course. In his case, he was single by choice. Going by what Vernon had said—

and the fact that she was living with the town matchmaker, Trudy felt differently.

Without Leah by his side, he should have found it easier to focus on the preaching, but instead he had to fight to keep his attention from wandering. Leah and Trudy were seated within view, and his eye kept drifting toward them.

Only because he wanted to make sure Leah was behaving properly, he told himself. She usually did behave herself in church, but she was so happy to be with Trudy, maybe she'd whisper or do something else she wasn't supposed to.

She didn't, not so far as he could tell. Trudy had given the child a handkerchief to play with, and Leah was amusing herself by folding it up into various shapes. At one point, when Leah got a little wiggly, Trudy took the handkerchief back. She flattened it on her lap and in a few quick folds created a tiny mouse, which she handed to a delighted Leah.

Leah examined the simple toy, smiling and gently swinging her legs back and forth as the preaching continued. Eli tried to refocus his attention on what the minister was saying, but it was a struggle.

He told himself it was because Leah looked so at ease, so comfortable that he couldn't tear his eyes away from her. But the truth was, he wasn't only looking at Leah.

His eyes kept straying to the woman sitting beside her.

Trudy clearly had a lot of experience caring for *kinder*. She glanced down at Leah now and again, but unlike Eli, she seemed to have no trouble keeping her mind on the service. Once, when Leah started swinging her feet a little too enthusiastically, Trudy reached down and gently touched the little girl's knee. When Leah looked up, startled, Trudy smiled and winked. Somehow Leah understood. Her legs went still, and she didn't seem upset at all.

He wondered again why Trudy hadn't married and started

a family of her own. She wasn't the prettiest woman in Hickory Springs, but that wasn't the most important thing. Besides, he liked how she looked. She had a bright, healthy appearance, a nice face and that sweet extra big smile.

Her hair was a real pretty color, too. Like the very best quality maple, it wasn't just one shade of brown, but a lot of them, all blended softly together. Such beautiful wood was a rare find, and it wasn't suited for anything ordinary. *Nee*, a smart craftsman saved such a piece to make something special, something sturdy and useful, but pretty, too.

Much like Trudy herself.

He was still studying Trudy's hair, thinking of what he'd make with wood of such a warm color, a trinket box, maybe, or a really nice rocker, when she glanced over and caught his eye. She didn't smile, but the corners of her eyes crinkled slightly, as if she didn't mind him looking at her.

Still he felt his cheeks getting hot. He quickly looked back at the minister, but it took him several minutes to gather his wits enough to follow the thread of the sermon.

After the service, Leah scampered over briefly to tell him that she wanted to sit with Trudy at lunch. Since the men and women sat at different tables, that worked well enough and saved Leah the sorrow of having to sit next to Vernon's *frau*, Jane—and Eli the sorrow of having to listen to her complain about it later.

It didn't, however, save Eli the aggravation of sitting next to Vernon. Trudy wasn't the only one who'd caught Eli looking.

"There's Charley if you need to speak to him." Vernon waved to the bishop with a grin. "Takes time to make wedding arrangements, you know. Better get things started."

Eli shot his *kossin* a hard look, but it was too late. The bishop headed in their direction.

Charley paused by the table and nodded pleasantly to the men. Then the bishop put a friendly hand on Eli's shoulder and bent to speak quietly in his ear.

"Looks like your visit to Susie's has paid off! I'm glad to see it, and I'll write to Jakob Hochstedler to let him know the matter's well on its way to being settled."

Startled, Eli glanced up at the bishop, but he had already moved on, and nobody else seemed to have heard the remark—although Vernon's eyes twinkled with humorous suspicion. No doubt Vernon had been joking with other folks, and that was why Charley had misunderstood Trudy's kind offer to look after Leah during church.

The conversation at the table had turned to the typical masculine topics of how the weather was impacting the fall crops and an upcoming charity auction over in Owl Hollow. Eli took another bite of soft white bread covered with the ever-present peanut butter church spread to avoid having to talk.

What was he going to do about this? Telling a bishop he was mistaken was a dicey business, and Eli was clumsier at talking than most. Still, he'd better set things straight soon, before the rumors reached Trudy's ears—or Leah's.

On the other hand, if Charley wrote to Jakob that Eli was involved in a courtship, the Carroway bishop would almost certainly drop the idea of taking Leah away. That was a tempting thought.

Would it be a sin to wait a while to explain the misunderstanding to Charley? At least long enough for that letter to be sent? *Probably so,* Eli thought gloomily. And when Charley found out there was no courtship going on after all, he wouldn't be pleased. Likely he'd write a very different letter to Jakob Hochstedler after that.

Eli rose from the table and headed out to hitch up the

buggy, trying to come up with some kind of a solution that wouldn't just make the situation worse. He was so deep in thought that he didn't hear Susie Raber calling until she was right behind him.

"Eli Mast," the older woman fussed breathlessly. "I've been chasing you all across the yard!"

"I'm sorry." Eli faced the matchmaker warily. "I was… thinking."

"About what? Trudy?" Susie put one hand on her hip and gave him a sharp look. "Oh, *ja*. I've heard about the goings on between the two of you. Come on. I want to talk to you."

She motioned him around to the side of the barn, out of the direct sight of the house. He followed after only the shortest hesitation. It wasn't like he had a choice. Judging by that expression on her face, she wouldn't turn him loose until she'd said her piece.

Susie walked to the very back corner of the building. Then she turned to face him, her face set in stern lines.

"I'm not pleased," Susie informed him. "As you can well imagine. Of course, Trudy's a grown woman, but she's living at my home. I don't think it speaks well of you that you'd start up a courtship behind my back." She cocked her head. "So? What do you have to say for yourself?"

Eli rubbed his jaw. This was getting out of hand. "That you're upset over nothing. Trudy's Leah's nanny, and that's all there is to it. No courtship's going on—it's nothing but gossip."

"Wait a minute." Susie frowned, studying him. "Are you saying you didn't ask Trudy if she was interested in a courtship with you? Because that's what she told me."

Trudy had told her? That stunned Eli into silence. After a few long seconds, he blinked and shook his head.

"*Nee*, I only asked if she was courting anybody else."

At least that was all he'd meant to ask. What had he said, exactly?

Susie narrowed her eyes. "Why would you ask any woman such a thing unless you were interested in courting her yourself?"

At least he knew the answer to that. "Because if she got married, she probably wouldn't work as a nanny anymore."

"Oh, my." Susie's expression shifted from suspicion to sympathy. "Trudy misunderstood. She thought that you..." The matchmaker shook her head. "Oh, my," she repeated sadly.

"Trudy thinks I wanted...that I was asking her..." So that was why she'd met him in the yard this morning and taken charge of Leah like she had. Because she thought... "I'm sorry. I didn't mean to give her the wrong idea."

"Well, you did, whether you meant to or not." Susie sighed. "But don't feel too badly. It's not all your fault. Trudy's been hoping for a husband for so long... I suppose when you started asking those questions, her hopes got the better of her, and she only heard what she wanted to hear."

Maybe, but his clumsy way with words probably hadn't helped matters. That realization made Eli irritable enough to say out loud what he'd been thinking ever since Trudy told him how long she'd been living at Susie's.

"Why's she been waiting so long, anyway? She's been with you for three months, she says. Why haven't you matched her up already? I see no reason why a nice girl like Trudy would be so hard to find a husband for, not if you know your business like folks say you do."

"The hard part's not finding her a husband. It's finding her the right husband." Susie looked thoughtfully at Eli. "Sounds like you think a good deal of Trudy."

"What I think about her doesn't matter."

"I don't know. It might." She studied him for a minute more. "It just might. Maybe I was a little too quick to send you on your way that day you came to see me."

He lifted an eyebrow. "I thought you said I wasn't ready for marriage."

"One step at a time. I'm still not saying you're ready for marriage. I'm saying you might be ready—possibly—for a courtship."

Eli frowned. "Doesn't one lead to the other?"

"Not always. Courtships fizzle out all the time." Susie chuckled. "Trust me, I know. Although sometimes it'll surprise you which ones end up sticking." She tilted her head thoughtfully. "And folks can learn plenty, even from the ones that don't work out. In this particular case, I think a few weeks of courting could do a lot of good—for the both of you."

Eli shook his head. "The only thing Trudy's likely to learn from courting me is that she never wants to get married at all."

Susie astonished him by nodding. "Maybe she'll learn that, *ja*. You see, the trouble is that Trudy's never been courted at all, so she's built up a lot of hopes and dreams about it." The matchmaker sighed. "It's the apple just out of reach that always looks the reddest, ain't so? That's true for men and women alike, so courting you might actually improve her prospects of marrying somebody else."

"Vass?" Was the woman making a joke? But Susie's face was perfectly serious.

"It's a funny thing, but once a fellow starts paying attention to a particular girl, other men often start paying attention, too, even if they never took notice of her before. As a matchmaker, I've seen it more times than I can count." She smiled. "The only apple that looks better than the one out of reach is the one in another fellow's hand, I guess."

"I guess." That seemed silly, but then he almost never understood how other people thought.

"Of course," she continued, "a courtship could be helpful to you, too. It would certainly get Bishop Coblentz off your back for a while—maybe long enough that this business about your niece would be forgotten."

Eli scratched his chin. So he wasn't the only one that had occurred to. He started to tell her about the bishop's earlier comment—then thought better of it.

"Oh, well. If you're not interested in a courtship with Trudy, none of that matters, does it? Since that's the case, best you straighten out this misunderstanding, and the sooner the better. The longer you put it off, the harder it'll be."

"Ja," Eli said slowly. "That's so. I'll deal with it."

Susie nodded as if satisfied by his answer, but she stood there for another minute, that strange thoughtful glint still in her eye. Finally, she sighed again.

"Well," she said. "Nobody's right all the time. Thankfully, *Gott* always knows how to turn our mistakes right side up."

"That's true enough," Eli answered absently, distracted by an idea slowly taking shape in his mind. "I keep Him plenty busy with my mistakes, certain sure."

"Oh, I wasn't talking about your mistake, Eli. I was talking about mine. But never mind. *Mach's gut,*" she said. "Be sure you talk to Trudy soon. Today, if you can manage it."

With that, she left him and headed back toward the Yoders' house.

Chapter Five

"Where did my *onkel* go?" Leah asked.

Trudy set the stack of plates she was carrying on the counter and glanced down at the little girl. The child didn't seem upset yet—only curious. But she had one finger in her mouth, which Trudy had learned meant Leah was growing uneasy.

"I don't know," Trudy answered honestly. "Probably outside with the other men. Why don't we go find him?"

Leah wasn't the only one who was getting *naerfich*. Trudy had been wondering where Eli had gotten off to. He'd done a disappearing act right after lunch before she had a chance to speak to him again.

Which—if she was being honest—was a little disappointing, especially after she'd caught him watching her during the service.

Of course, she'd not expected Eli to make a show of the fact they were courting, not in front of people and certainly not at church. But... Trudy's eyes drifted over to the corner of the yard where Lina Yoder and Andy Miller were talking and exchanging long meaningful looks.

No official announcement had been made yet, but Lina's shy blushes and the fact that Andy couldn't stay more than a couple of yards away from her told their secret as clear as day. Plainly the two had become a couple. No doubt there would soon be an announcement in church and a wedding shortly afterward.

Trudy was happy for them, but she had secretly hoped that today it would be her turn to cause a ripple of friendly gossip. The morning had started off so promisingly, with their conversation in the yard and that long look in church, but since then Eli had barely spoken to her.

She threaded her way through the busy kitchen leading Leah toward the back door. Anna Weaver stood beside it, chatting with Susie, who'd apparently just come back in from outside. Anna smiled as Trudy and Leah joined them.

"Susie and I are talking about the bidding picnic that's being planned to raise the money for poor Caleb King's final medical bills. We've never had anything like it here in Hickory Springs before, and everybody's real interested to see how it goes."

"A bidding picnic? I've never heard of such a thing."

"Women pack up picnic baskets and folks bid on them," Anna explained. "Marlene Smucker came up with the idea. She has a *kossin* who married a Mennonite, and they do them all the time." She glanced down at Leah and smiled. "I see you've got a new friend today, Trudy," Anna said, a lilt of friendly curiosity in her voice.

"Trudy is Leah's nanny." Susie's tone was so matter-of-fact that the teasing glimmer faded from Anna's eye.

"Oh! That's nice," she responded pleasantly.

"It is. *Very* nice." Trudy shot Susie a narrow look as she edged past them toward the door.

Susie knew quite well that her relationship with Eli had turned into more than just a job. *Ja*, courtships were supposed to be kept secret, especially at the start, but people did tend to guess, and Trudy had seen Susie dropping hints before about courting couples. A knowing nod, a half smile... People knew what those little signs meant.

Trudy knew it was selfish to seek attention, but she'd so been looking forward to finally being part of a new couple that people were guessing about. Even though Susie didn't approve of this courtship, would it have hurt for her to hint— just a little—that Trudy's relationship with Eli and Leah was more than just a nanny job?

Still slightly annoyed, she walked across the Yoders' sun-dappled yard, Leah in tow. Sure enough, Eli was in front of the barn, hitching up his buggy. At the sight of her beloved *onkel*, Leah tugged happily at Trudy's arm, urging her to walk faster.

However, Trudy refused to be hurried, warily considering the frown on Eli's face. He didn't look pleased, and suddenly she didn't feel nearly so eager to talk to him.

When they were a few steps away, Leah let go of her hand and hurried to Eli, who swung her easily up into his arms. He gave his niece a brief smile and a hug before setting her up on the buggy seat.

"Wait right there," he told the little girl. "I'll have us ready to leave in a few minutes."

Trudy remained where she was, feeling more and more uncomfortable. Wasn't Eli even going to speak to her? Should she speak first? She had no idea.

A few seconds later, Eli finished hooking up the lines and turned to face her.

"I need to talk to you about something." He looked resigned, like a man faced with a particularly difficult task.

"All right," she answered lightly. "What?"

He threw a cautious look at Leah, swinging her feet on the buggy seat. She was absorbed in watching a trio of bright cardinals squabbling at a bird feeder, so he stepped a few steps farther away, out of earshot.

Trudy followed and faced him, fingers clenched together and her mouth dry as paper.

Eli cleared his throat. "The other day on the porch when we were talking…"

Trudy's heart skittered out of rhythm. *"Ja?"*

"I asked if you were interested in a fellow. If you were planning to get married anytime soon." He kicked at a rock on the ground.

"You did," Trudy said finally. "And I answered you honestly."

"I know." He shot her a quick uncertain look. "The trouble is, I'm not so *gut* at talking to people. Sometimes I say things backward, and people get the wrong idea."

"Oh." Trudy felt blood draining from her cheeks. "And you think you gave me the wrong idea about something?"

"It seems so." He kicked at the rock again. "Did you really think I was asking because I was interested in courting you myself?"

Did you really think?

Those four words rendered Trudy unable to think at all.

She'd been wrong. She'd been so sure…but somehow she'd misunderstood.

She didn't know what to say, so finally, desperately, she answered his question with one of her own. "Why *did* you ask?"

His answer came fast and sure—and plain as day. "If you were planning to get married soon, you'd not be able to keep a nannying job, likely. That would have meant another change for Leah, and she doesn't do so well with changes."

He'd only asked if Trudy was courting somebody because of Leah. Not because he was interested in courting her himself. Of course, he wasn't. Nobody had ever been interested in courting her.

"Oh! I see." She nodded—a few too many times.

He'd quit kicking the rock and was watching her, a muscle working in his jaw as if he was chewing on the inside of his cheek. "Did you think different, Trudy? Did I...say things backward and give you the wrong idea?"

Trudy was suddenly aware that there were people still milling about—no doubt noticing she and Eli standing together and talking. The bishop's wife herself, Martha Coblentz, was just walking down the porch steps. The woman caught Trudy's eye and smiled, happy speculation plain on her round face. Trudy looked away quickly.

Martha was a dear, sweet woman who loved to spread good news. If she thought Trudy and Eli were interested in each other, she'd tell it far and wide. And later—when it was clear that no courtship was going on—there'd be lots of pitying glances. And maybe a few knowing chuckles from the menfolk, quickly hushed by their wives. No doubt, she'd be asked to somebody's house for a sympathy dinner.

Again.

There'd also be Susie to deal with. She was far too kind to say *I told you so*, but she could hardly be faulted for thinking it.

"Well?" Eli prompted, throwing another wary look toward Leah. The cardinals had fluttered away from the feeder to continue their fussing elsewhere, and the little girl was looking in their direction curiously. "Did I give you the wrong idea or not?"

Somehow that blunt question was the last straw. Not only had she been plucked from the giddy heights of her first real courtship right back into Good Apple Girl status, but now he wanted her to admit out loud how silly she'd been, right here in the Yoders' side yard.

Since there didn't seem to be any way out of it, she squared her shoulders and made herself look him in the eye.

"If I did misunderstand you," she said, keeping her voice low, "such a thing would be plenty embarrassing enough without you putting me on the spot about it at a church gathering. Wouldn't it have been kinder to ask me about this later? In private?"

"Ach!" The horrified expression on his face would have been funny, if Trudy hadn't been well past the point of seeing humor in anything. "I should have," he muttered. "I just... I wanted to get this over with, and I didn't think. Like I told you, I'm no good at this."

"You're right about that," Trudy agreed, too weary to worry about being polite. "But never mind. We understand each other now."

Miserably, she turned away and started back toward the house.

"Wait!"

Trudy stopped and stood with her back to him for a second. Smarter to keep going. She'd been humiliated enough already.

But somehow she couldn't move. Finally, reluctantly, she looked over her shoulder at him.

That must have been the invitation Eli was waiting for, because he closed the gap between them in a couple of strides.

"I'm sorry, Trudy. I've made a muck of this." He took off his hat and ran an impatient hand through his dark hair, ruffling it up. "That's what I do. Whenever I try to make things better, I generally end up making them worse, so all I know to do is talk to you straight. It's true that I wasn't asking about a courtship before, not like you thought." He looked down at her, and that muscle in his jaw jumped again. "But I'm asking you now."

Eli held his breath and waited for Trudy to say something. But she didn't. She only stared at him, wide-eyed.

She seemed to be having some trouble making sense of this. He could hardly blame her. He could barely make sense out of it himself.

Susie had put the idea in his head when she'd pointed out that a courtship wasn't the same thing as a marriage. That was so. At the start, it was just two people spending time together to see if they could be compatible life partners. Sometimes that led to marriage—mostly, it seemed. Then again, Susie had said that plenty of courtships came to nothing, and she ought to know.

And then there was what she'd said about Trudy—how she wanted a courtship so bad that she'd misunderstood him. Now he wasn't so sure that was all Trudy's fault. Probably he'd asked the question wrong. He usually did.

But still it bothered him. He hadn't liked the idea of Trudy being embarrassed or disappointed—although, of course, he'd only made it worse trying to straighten it out.

So, he'd thought, if Trudy was so anxious for a courtship as everyone seemed to think, why shouldn't he give her one? He knew it wouldn't amount to much. Trudy was a bright woman. In a few weeks, she was sure to realize that Eli wasn't the *mann* for her and put an end to it.

And maybe it really would make some other fellow take notice of her, like Susie said. Although, Eli wasn't so sure. That nonsense Susie had talked about—about how some men thought apples looked better in another man's hand— he didn't think much of that.

A *schmaert* man knew a good apple when he saw it.

And, of course, he had his own reasons, too. There was no getting around the fact that courting Trudy would help him out. Especially since Charley already believed a courtship was going on.

"Are we going soon, *Onkel*?" Leah called restlessly from the buggy.

"*Ja*, just a minute," he called over his shoulder. He looked back at Trudy who still appeared stunned.

"I..." She blinked twice and shrugged helplessly. "Eli, I don't know what to say."

That made two of them, and there was no time to figure it out now. Leah was growing impatient, and men were moving toward the barn to hitch up buggies and start their treks homeward. Trudy was right. This was no place for a private talk. He should have known that.

As if to prove Trudy's point, Charley Coblentz passed by on his way to collect his horse. The bishop caught Eli's eye and gave an approving nod.

"If you're not interested—" Eli started.

"*Nee*, I..." Trudy's cheeks flushed a darker pink. "I'm not saying that. I... I'm interested. I just think this isn't the best time to talk about it."

"*Gut*." He'd better beat a hasty retreat before he messed this up more than he had already. "That's settled, then. We'll fix up the details later on." Without waiting for an answer, he hurried back to join Leah in the buggy.

His heart was still hammering as they clopped onto the road, leaving the Yoders' house behind them.

Leah looked up at him curiously. "What were you and Trudy talking about for so long?"

"Just something we needed to settle between us." He glanced down at the little girl. "You like Trudy, *ja*?"

"I love Trudy!" There was no mistaking the enthusiasm in Leah's voice. "I can't wait to see her tomorrow morning!"

Tomorrow morning. Eli's stomach clenched itself into a knot. That's right. He'd be dropping Leah off at Susie Raber's bright and early tomorrow morning. He might be able to dodge a conversation then—he had his work to get to, after all. The afternoon would be harder. Trudy would be expecting a courtship, and he had no idea how to go about that.

Likely, he'd say all the wrong things, like he usually did. And if he wasn't saying the wrong things, he was doing them, which was even worse.

Eli sighed and flicked the reins on Star's back. *Ja*, if Trudy had half as much sense as he thought she did, this courtship would be over before it even began.

Chapter Six

"How's that chair coming?"

Eli stopped pedaling the lathe, and the chair leg he was smoothing spun slowly to a halt. He sighed. It was only half past eight in the morning, but he'd been working for two hours already.

"It's coming," he said shortly. He hoped Vernon didn't plan to hang around. He had too much work to do, and he had no intention of staying late again this afternoon.

He hadn't seen Trudy for two days—not since their conversation on Sunday.

When he'd arrived home that afternoon, Vernon had been in a dither about how far behind they were filling orders. This was the downside to adding so many new *Englisch* customers. More work than time, and customers who weren't particularly patient.

Sunday wasn't a day for discussing work, so Vernon had kept the conversation short, but he'd asked Eli to work some overtime this week so they could catch up.

"If we go in early and stay late for a few days, we can get things moving," his *kossin* had said. "And don't worry about Leah. Jane can drive her to and from Trudy's for you."

Eli hadn't liked the plan—and he'd known Leah wouldn't like it, either. They enjoyed their morning and evening buggy rides together, and his niece and Jane Flaud had never really hit it off.

Then there was Trudy. He'd been *naerfich* about seeing her Monday, but leaving their courtship conversation hanging didn't seem like a good idea, either.

His vague protests were overruled by Vernon, who saw no reason why his plan wouldn't work perfectly fine. Eli couldn't explain without letting on about the change in his and Trudy's relationship—and he wasn't looking forward to his *kossin* ribbing him about that.

Not that it was likely to be a secret for long. Several people had noticed Eli and Trudy together in the Yoders' yard after church, and such news got around fast.

"I appreciate the extra work you've put in," Vernon said now. "That table and chair set's near done. If we keep this up the rest of the week—"

"I'll get them finished, but I'm not working late today," Eli interrupted. "I want to pick Leah up myself. She wasn't feeling too well this morning, and I want to check with Trudy and see how she did today."

That much was true. Leah hadn't acted like herself at all. Eli suspected the child's downcast mood had something to do with the prospect of another morning buggy ride with the stern-faced Jane, but he kept that to himself.

Vernon slanted a teasing look in his direction. "Well, Trudy will sure be glad to see you. Jane's been saying how disappointed she looks when she sees you're not the one driving the buggy." He winked. "Poor girl, no doubt she thought she'd finally found herself a husband, and then you go and disappear on her."

Poor girl.

Eli felt a flash of annoyance. "Trudy's not anybody's poor

girl," he said. "I wish you wouldn't joke about her like that. She's been a real big help to me with Leah."

His *kossin* looked at Eli with a sharp interest. "Sorry. I didn't mean anything by it. I think Trudy's a real nice person. Nothing wrong with her. I guess some women are just made to be single."

"Maybe so." Eli's eye drifted over to the maple board he'd found in Vernon's scrap shed yesterday. "Although I don't see why everybody's so sure Trudy's one of them." When Vernon lifted an eyebrow, Eli shrugged irritably. "I don't see the problem. She's a faithful member of the church and a hard worker. She's sure got a knack with little ones, and a pleasant temper near as I can tell."

"True, and those are fine things. They just aren't what young fellows think about first when it comes to courting."

"Seems most of them don't think at all."

Vernon chuckled. "Maybe not, but who can blame them? When a fellow meets the girl that's meant for him, his mind tends to get muddled up. At least that's how it was with me when I first took notice of Jane. Couldn't think straight for months. And whenever I wasn't with her I was as grumpy as a cat with a sore tail. Sort of like you are right now." He winked—then clapped his hands abruptly. "Well, it's time to open up the store. And you'd better get back to work on that chair if you aren't planning on working late."

His *kossin* walked back into the showroom. Eli turned back to his lathe, mulling over the conversation with a feeling of disbelief.

It just made no sense to him how other men picked their wives. Why should a woman like Jane be chosen, and Trudy overlooked? Jane was a trim, efficient woman, a hard worker and a passable cook. All good qualities, but Eli saw nothing about her that would muddle a man's thinking.

Jane didn't have a smile like Trudy's, one that lit up her whole face, or a quick bubbly laugh. And Jane's hair was the color of straw. Not that there was anything wrong with that, but it couldn't hold a candle to Trudy's rich, warm brown.

As he set the lathe turning again, he glanced again at the plank of maple wood he'd finally chosen from the odds and ends in Vernon's storage shed—after examining at least a dozen others during his lunch break yesterday.

It wasn't exactly the color of Trudy's hair, but it was close. With a bit of polishing up and the right stain, he could get it even closer. He thought maybe he'd make a little gift for Trudy out of it. That seemed like the sort of thing a fellow might do for a girl he was courting.

Not that he knew much about it. He'd no idea what to make, either. He considered various possibilities as he worked through his day, but he couldn't come to a decision.

At five o'clock on the dot, he put down his tools and picked up the piece of maple on his way out the door. He'd take it along with him. He'd show it to Trudy and ask her straight out what she'd like best. A box, maybe, that she could keep little things in. Hairpins and other such bits and pieces.

Ja, a nice box with a snug, clever lid that wouldn't get knocked off too easy. That would be a practical gift.

Still, he'd better check and make sure. A lot of women didn't seem to care much for practical things.

Or practical men.

Trudy tried her best to be quiet as she finished straightening up the living room. She tiptoed across the floor, putting the storybook she'd been reading to Leah back on its shelf and gathering the crayons and paper she'd encouraged the child to use.

Nothing had held Leah's attention. She wasn't feeling well.

She was napping now on the sofa, covered with an old quilt, and snoring softly, a half-empty cup of lemon ginger tea on a nearby table.

Apparently, the poor child had caught the cold that was going around the community. She'd seemed slightly off this morning, and by midafternoon was congested and complaining of a sore throat. Nothing too alarming, thankfully. As a nanny, Trudy had seen plenty of head colds, and Leah seemed only uncomfortable and a bit droopy.

Still, she'd need to let Eli know, and that was a problem. She'd not laid eyes on him since their conversation at church.

She'd come home from the Yoders' with such high hopes. She'd spent the rest of her Sunday daydreaming about seeing Eli on Monday, wondering how this new romance between them would start.

Would he suggest a buggy ride or a walk? Invite her to lunch on Saturday, maybe? Bring her a thoughtful gift, like a little bag of candy? Amish men mostly didn't give such presents, but one of her sister's special friends had, and Trudy had thought it very sweet.

On Monday morning, she'd worn her favorite dress and waited, heart pounding, for Eli to bring Leah. But instead, Jane Flaud had dropped Leah off, explaining in her brisk way that Eli was very busy at work and that she'd be driving Leah for the time being.

Trudy had nodded and smiled, trying to hide her disappointment. But the more she thought about it, the worse she felt.

Maybe she'd never been courted herself, but she'd had a front-row seat to her sisters' courtships—and for that matter, her brothers'. She'd never seen a boy let anything keep him away from a girl who'd caught his eye for long, especially not when things were first getting started.

Then again, she kept reminding herself, Eli wasn't a boy. He was a man, with a man's responsibilities and a child to look after. He had to take his work seriously.

Maybe that's all this was. Just a little delay. But still, her feelings felt bruised, and she couldn't help wondering if Eli was really interested in her. Maybe he'd only asked if she'd be interested in courting out of kindness—because she'd embarrassed herself by misunderstanding him that first time.

After tucking the quilt more snugly around Leah's shoulders, Trudy slipped out to the kitchen. Susie, another victim of the cold, had stayed home from the bakery and was sitting at the table drinking her own cup of lemon ginger tea.

She watched as Trudy rummaged in a drawer for a pad and pencil. "What are you doing?"

"Writing a note for Jane to take to back Eli. I have to tell him about Leah's cold."

"So Eli's still tied up at work?" Susie took another cautious sip of her steaming tea. "Vernon must be a demanding boss."

"Mmm." Trudy kept her eyes on the notepad she and Susie used for their grocery lists. She'd not explained to Susie about how she'd misunderstood Eli's point at first. She hadn't figured it mattered now, since Eli had asked her to consider a courtship, after all.

"Well, it's *gut* that Eli's a hard worker. That's an important quality," Susie said. But then she added, "But it's not the only important one. And it's awful hard to get to know a fellow if you never get to spend any time with him. Any idea when he'll be coming by?"

"As soon as he can, I'm sure," Trudy answered—which

wasn't entirely truthful. She wasn't a bit sure, but she didn't want to admit that to Susie.

Susie coughed and set her teacup back into its saucer. "While you have the notepad out, add honey to the grocery list. Our jar's almost empty. I just hope Lydia Riehl has dropped more off at Anna's store, because she was nearly out last time I was there. With all these colds going around, honey's in short supply."

"All right."

Susie dabbed at her nose. "And stop fretting. If he's serious about courting you, Eli's bound to show up sooner or later."

Trudy bit her lip. "Do you think he's serious, Susie?" Surely, a matchmaker would be able to tell, one way or the other.

"I don't know. And neither do you, not yet. How a man acts tells you a lot more than what he says. You have to see how he behaves, how he treats you. That'll tell you everything you need to know. Now, add that honey to our list before you forget."

As Trudy flipped over a page and added honey to their ongoing list, the noise of a horse and buggy rolling into the yard made both women glance toward the back door.

"That'll be Jane," Trudy said. "I'd better go wake Leah."

"It's not Jane." Susie had risen and was craning her neck to peek out the kitchen window. "It's Eli." She glanced back at Trudy and smiled. "Why don't you let the child sleep a few extra minutes so you two can talk?" Susie took her teacup to the sink. "I'm suddenly feeling a little tired myself," she added with a wink. "I think I'll go upstairs and rest for a few minutes. But I'll hear if Leah calls out."

Trudy's heart was pounding so hard that she barely heard her. Eli was finally here, and surely that meant their courtship was about to get started. No doubt he'd be asking her to go on a buggy ride some afternoon or maybe to get a slice of pie at the café.

She wondered what he would suggest first. Not that it mattered. Whatever it was, she'd agree.

She checked to make sure Leah was still sound asleep—and then walked outside.

The September afternoon seemed brighter than it had only a few minutes ago. The sky was a sharp autumn blue, dotted with fluffy clouds so white they looked as if they'd been bleached. A playful breeze ruffled the golden leaves, bringing the whiff of a neighbor's bonfire to Trudy's nose.

Eli jumped out of the buggy, but instead of heading for the house, he paused to reach into the rear seat for something.

Trudy clasped her hands together, feeling a sense of happy anticipation. If Eli had brought her some little gift, well—then, as Susie said, she'd know. She'd know for certain sure that he was serious about their courtship.

That he was serious about *her*.

But as she watched, Eli pulled out a thick plank of wood. Trudy's smile faded as he hefted it easily and started walking toward the house, the board balanced over his shoulder like a seesaw.

Why on earth had he brought along a plank? A big one, too, although its weight didn't seem to bother him in the slightest. He held the board in place casually, one hand splayed over its lower half.

"Hello, Trudy," he said, as he neared the steps. *"Vi bisht du?"*

As he spoke, he slid the board off his shoulder. Only the muscles rippling under the blue fabric of his shirtsleeves betrayed how heavy the piece was. Likely, she couldn't have lifted it at all.

"Trudy?"

She blinked. He'd asked her a question.

"I'm fine, *denki*. But I'm afraid that Leah's sick."

"Sick?" Eli's expression shifted from mild puzzlement to alarm. "I thought she didn't act quite herself this morning. What kind of sick?"

"Nothing bad, just the cold that's going around. Susie has it, too. I don't think Leah needs the doctor, but she might need some medicine if she starts feeling worse. Anna Weaver keeps some natural cold remedies at her shop, so you might check in there."

"I'll do that." Frowning, he picked up the plank and started up the steps. Trudy stepped aside so he could pass, eyeing the board curiously.

"Eli? What's that?"

"It's maple." Inside the kitchen, Eli leaned the plank carefully against the wall. "I brought it for you, if you want it. We can talk about it later. Where's Leah?"

"Asleep on the couch." He'd brought her a board? Why? Thoroughly confused, Trudy followed Eli into the living room.

He halted just inside the doorway, his gaze fixed on the small figure curled on the couch. *"Ach,"* he murmured miserably. "She must be really sick. She never sleeps during the day."

"Rest is the best thing for her. That and lots of liquids. I've got a jar of Susie's chicken soup that you can warm up for her supper. It'll do her a world of good."

Eli walked to the couch and leaned down to lay one hand gently over the sleeping child's forehead. "She feels warm."

"She would, underneath that blanket. I don't think she's

running a fever, but if she is, it's just her body doing its job to fight off the germs. She'll be right as rain in a few days."

"I hope so." He gathered the child in his arms, quilt and all. Leah stirred slightly.

"Onkel?" she murmured with a sniffle.

"Ja, it's me. Trudy tells me you're not feeling so *gut."* He glanced at Trudy. "Can I take the quilt with us? I'd like to keep her good and warm on the ride. It's not cold, but there's some wind. I'll bring it back."

"Of course." Trudy pushed back her disappointment. Clearly, any courtship plans would have to wait for another day—along with the explanation about that board in Susie's kitchen. "I'll get the soup and carry it out to the buggy for you."

"Denki."

In the kitchen, she gathered up the mason jar of homemade chicken soup, a fresh loaf of sourdough bread and some sugar cookies that Susie had kindly donated. She tucked the simple supper in a basket and covered it with a napkin—and threw another puzzled glance at the board as she passed it on her way to the door.

When she reached the buggy, Eli had just finished tucking Leah in the back seat. He hurried to take the basket from her.

"Denki," he said. "For the food, and the loan of the quilt. But mostly for taking such good care of Leah."

"I was glad to do it."

He nodded, his dark eyes worried. "It's a comfort to know that she was well looked after when she wasn't feeling well. She's been sick only a handful of times, and I'm never certain I know the right things to do."

"There's no need to worry. Children usually shake these things fast. Feed her the soup and give her a cup of chamomile tea before bed with a big dollop of honey. That'll soothe her throat. A good night's sleep and she may feel much better in the morning."

"I'll do that." Eli hesitated, as if he were going to say something else. Maybe, Trudy thought hopefully, he'd say something about their courtship plans, after all. Or at least explain that ridiculous board.

But before he could speak, a muffled sneeze sounded under the quilt.

Eli looked over his shoulder. "I'd best get her home out of the chill. *Mach's gut*, Trudy," he said. "Please give Susie my thanks for the food."

He swung up into the seat and clucked to his horse. As the buggy rattled onto the highway, Trudy walked slowly back to the house, her sense of disappointment growing with every step.

Eli had been nice and very appreciative, but he hadn't said anything—not one thing—that any of her former employers mightn't have said to her. She knew he was worried about Leah, but still.

It was discouraging.

Susie appeared in the doorway, holding a fresh box of tissues. "Eli didn't stay long."

"*Nee*, he didn't," Trudy said shortly.

Susie gave her a sympathetic look. "Well, Trudy, I—" She stopped short and frowned. "What's that?" She pointed at the board.

"Eli brought it."

"He did? Why?"

"I have no idea." Trudy went to the sink to begin the process of washing up the teacups and sticky spoons. She glanced through the window and decided the afternoon wasn't that pretty, after all.

Susie considered the board with a perplexed look. "You didn't ask?"

"*Nee*, I didn't." Trudy squirted dishwashing liquid into the sink. "All he said was that it was maple. And that it was for me."

"For you." Susie walked closer and touched the board with a tentative finger. "That's all he said?" She glanced at Trudy, her face thoughtful. "I know I've told you this before, but you really should ask more questions, Trudy."

The older woman stood there, studying the board for another moment. "You know," she said finally. "Lydia Riehl usually delivers her honey on Fridays. Why don't you ask Eli to drive you to the store that afternoon? I'll stay here with Leah, so you two can have some time alone."

"I'm not sure Eli wants to spend any time alone with me, Susie." Trudy wiped a smudge off a spoon with some force. "You said I'd be able to tell if he was serious about this courtship by how he behaved, and you were right. It seems pretty clear." She rinsed the cup and set it in the drainer. "He stays away for two days, and when he finally comes by, he hurries off after hardly speaking to me." She gave a hard little shrug. "I know Leah wasn't feeling well, but it's only a cold—nothing to be so worried over. I think he just didn't want to talk to me."

"You might be right, Trudy." Susie tilted her head thoughtfully. "Then again, you might not. With some men, you never know unless you ask. Take my advice—for once. Gather up your courage, go on that buggy ride and ask Eli straight out why he brought this board to you. I think it might be important."

"It's a board, Susie." Exasperated, Trudy turned away from the sink to stare at her friend. "How important could it possibly be?"

"I'm not sure." Susie traced a finger along the swirling grain of the wood. "That's what makes it so interesting." She glanced at Trudy and smiled. "Life's just full of surprises, and your Eli's shaping up to be the biggest one I've had in quite a while. Now, take care with that dishcloth! You're dripping soapy water all over the floor."

Picking up her box of tissues, Susie headed back up the stairs to her room.

Chapter Seven

The following Friday afternoon, Eli flicked the reins on Star's back, but the gelding barely increased his pace. The horse wasn't enthusiastic about this trip out to Anna Weaver's store in a cold autumn rain.

Eli glanced to the side where Trudy sat on the buggy seat, her hands clasped in her lap, her black bonnet framing her face. She caught his eye and smiled. Eli quickly looked away and flicked the reins again.

"Get up, Star," he said.

The horse snorted and grudgingly sped up. Every step was taking the horse farther from his warm stall, and he didn't plan on going any faster than he had to.

That was a problem because Eli wanted to get this trip over with quickly. Not that he minded driving Trudy to the store for honey or whatever else she wanted. But she'd expect him to talk to her on the way, and that's where things got tricky.

Driving on the roads in such awful weather was distracting, and being with Trudy was already distracting enough. If he talked much at all, there was no telling what a muddle he could make between here and the Weavers' farm.

"I could go on my own," he'd offered when he arrived

at Susie's that afternoon. "And bring the honey back. It's spitting rain out today, and the wind's blowing it sideways."

He hadn't missed the sympathetic look Susie had given Trudy, or the flash of hurt in Trudy's eyes. He'd said the wrong thing, as usual. But also, as usual, he had no idea *why* it was wrong.

"*Nee*, I'd better come along," Trudy had insisted lightly. "If Anna doesn't have any of Lydia Riehl's honey in, I'll need to pick out something else."

"Oh." A reassuring idea had occurred to him, and he'd added with some relief, "The Farmhouse Pantry's not so far, so maybe the drive won't take long, even in the rain."

The women had exchanged another exasperated look, and Eli had winced. Clearly, the safest thing for him to do was not to say much else, so since then he'd kept his mouth shut and let Trudy do the talking.

And talk she had…about the weather, Leah's day—how she was already feeling much better and looking forward to baking cookies with Susie while they ran their errand. About how many people in the community were down with the cold that was going around, and how Lydia Riehl's honey was so good because she'd learned all about beekeeping from old Mattie Kauffman.

He listened and nodded—nods were safer than words. Now and then when Trudy left a silence stretching out too long, he made a thoughtful humming noise, hoping that would encourage her to keep talking.

It usually did, and he was glad. He wanted her to keep talking, and not only because it got him off the hook for coming up with something to say himself. He liked listening to her chatter.

Growing up with his *aent*, the remarks he'd most often heard during a buggy ride were criticisms about the farms they passed, the other buggies, even the people she saw walking along the sidewalk. Oh, Lora Mast had called her comments concern, but judgment was at the root of it. His *aent* could find something to "worry" about in pretty much everyone she met.

Trudy's talk was far more pleasant. She found something nice to say about everything and everybody. Like that day when she'd come to see him about the nanny job, when they'd walked to the park. She'd talked about the clouds, he remembered, about how pretty they were.

He liked that, much the way he liked watching Leah wonder over simple things like frogs or flowers. Like the child's fresh delight in the world, Trudy's cheerful talk made him notice and appreciate those things more himself.

That was real nice, and with all his heart, he wished he could find some way to return the favor. But nothing he said ever seemed to come out quite right.

Nowadays, he usually didn't fret over his stumbles much. There wasn't much point in minding things you couldn't help no matter how hard you tried. But he minded about Trudy. He didn't like seeing that spark of hurt in her eyes over something he'd clumsily said or done.

Nee, he didn't like that one bit.

"Do you have any special plans this week?" she asked now.

"*Nee*, nothing special."

"Oh."

As another pause stretched out between them, he noticed an odd scraping sound. He tensed and tilted his head, listening. Unless he missed his guess, something was going wrong with one of the buggy wheels.

"I don't have anything much going on, either," Trudy was saying.

He nodded, but his attention was riveted on the noise. *Ja*, there was definitely something going on with a wheel. Sounded like a metal band might be coming loose.

"There's an auction over in Owl Hollow on Saturday. Did you hear about it? It's a fundraiser to help one of their families raise money for medical expenses. A lot of their people have donated items, and our district took a wagonload over, too. I think it might be fun."

It was the back left wheel, Eli decided. He'd better check it. *"Ja,"* he answered absently. "I heard about that auction. There's supposed to be some woodworking tools going up for sale, so I'm planning to drive over and check it out. If they're as nice as I think they are, I'll bid on them."

"Oh. Are you going with Vernon?"

"Nee, I'm going on my own. Vernon's more shopkeeper than woodworker these days."

"I see." Trudy sounded disappointed. He must have put a foot wrong again, although why she'd care that Vernon preferred to work behind a counter, he couldn't imagine.

In any case, he'd have to figure that out later. The scraping sound was getting worse.

Eli pulled the buggy over to the side of the road and held the reins out in Trudy's direction. "Take these a minute. Something needs checking."

Once she accepted the reins, he jumped out of the buggy into the rain and walked around to inspect the wheel. As he'd suspected, a piece of the metal band on the wheel had come loose and was dragging. When he wiggled it, the section came off in his hand.

He made a disgusted noise. Of all things to happen when he was driving Trudy in such poor weather.

He walked back around and tossed the scrap of metal into

the back of the buggy before climbing back into his seat. He reached over and reclaimed the reins.

"Sorry," he said. "To make you sit and wait. And in this rain, too." He flicked the reins irritably and clucked to the horse. "Get up, Star!"

"Was something wrong?"

"Ja." He mentally calculated how far they were from the Weavers'. Not far, he realized with some relief. He needed to take a closer look at that wheel, but he wanted to get Trudy safely out of the weather first.

"Well?" Trudy prompted sharply. Surprised, he glanced over at her. She looked back at him, her mouth pressed into a tight line. When he didn't answer, she shook her head— an impatient shake that sent raindrops splattering on him. "What's wrong with the buggy, Eli?"

"Part of the metal band's coming off one wheel." Likely she was worried about being stranded in the poor weather. And who could blame her? "But it should get us to the Weavers' farm and home again. I'll make sure of it while you do your shopping. It shouldn't delay us much."

He figured that ought to reassure her. Maybe it did because Trudy didn't say another word until they arrived at the Farmhouse Pantry.

He drove up as close to the small store building as he could, so that Trudy had as few steps as possible to get inside. A warm light glowed in the store windows, and the open sign was hanging on its wooden post, so Anna Weaver must be inside.

"Go on in and get your honey and whatever else you need. I'm going to drive around to the barn and get a better look at this wheel." As he spoke, Jeremiah Weaver stepped to the big open doorway of the barn and raised a hand in greeting. Eli waved back. "There's Jeremiah. I'll have him take a look at it, too."

Trudy sighed. "All right." She twisted around to begin the process of climbing down out of the buggy.

"Mind yourself now. Everything's slick with the rain."

He'd have rather set the brake and gone round to help her, but he wanted to catch Jeremiah at the barn. He'd like the farmer's opinion on the wheel before he started back. He'd not have worried about it if he'd been alone, but he didn't like the idea of having wheel trouble with Trudy in the buggy, not in this weather.

He waited until she vanished into the shelter of the store. Then he drove the short distance to the barn where Jeremiah promptly agreed to help him check over the wheel.

Jeremiah Weaver was a farmer now, but he'd spent years as a delivery driver, so he'd dealt with plenty of wheel problems. He assessed the damaged wheel with an experienced eye and agreed with Eli's opinion that it was safe to drive home on.

"You'll want to get it fixed soon, though," Jeremiah said.

"*Ja*, and it isn't something I can do myself." Fixing wheels required a very specialized set of skills. "Any wheelwrights around here you'd recommend?"

"Only one, and that's Jonas Stoll. He does *gut* work, and he can use the money, what with his boy being sick and all."

"*Denki*. I'll speak to him." Eli glanced toward the store. "I left Trudy Schwartz with your Anna. I guess I'd better go collect her now that I'm sure of this wheel."

"Ah, you brought Trudy?" Jeremiah gave a matter-of-fact nod. "She's a nice girl. Anna's always glad to see her."

That was all he said. People didn't usually comment much on courtships. It was considered best to let a couple work such decisions out between themselves and *Gott*. But the community was aware when a man and a woman started taking special notice of each other, and they had their ways of making opinions known.

Jeremiah was sending the same message the bishop had when he'd passed by and given that approving nod. Trudy was a good choice.

Back in Carroway, once his years as a bachelor had stretched out past the usual limit, people found lots of opportunities to praise various girls in front of him. Clearly, they thought he should get married, like all young men were expected to do. That was one of the hard things about being Plain. Everybody was expected to fit into the same church-approved mold—whether they were suited to it or not.

Their not-so-subtle hints had only made Eli feel squirrelly, as if he was wearing a shirt that was too tight around the neck.

But Jeremiah's remark didn't make him feel uncomfortable at all, and not just because he didn't expect this courtship to end in a marriage. He was glad, he realized as he climbed back into the buggy seat. Glad the Weavers liked Trudy and spoke well of her. She deserved that. Because she really was a very nice girl.

"*Mach's gut*, Jeremiah," he called over his shoulder. The tall man nodded and then turned back to his own work.

Eli drove back up to the store and set the brake. The rain was coming down harder now, rattling heavily on the tin roof of the building. Unlikely Trudy would hear him pull up.

That was all right. Trudy had only mentioned buying honey, but she might have picked up some other things as well. He didn't want her trying to carry heavy bundles out to the buggy, not with the ground all slippery and wet. He'd best go in and carry things for her. Besides, she'd not taken an umbrella, and he had a big one stowed behind the seat.

He fished around for it and then jumped down from the buggy and started up the path to the store.

He heard the women's voices just as he reached the shelter of the overhang in front of the door. He wasn't planning to listen. He only paused to fold up the umbrella so as not to splash any more water than necessary on Anna's floor.

But then he heard his name.

"I don't think Eli's really interested in courting me at all, Anna," Trudy was saying unhappily. "I suppose that's no big surprise." A short sad laugh. "No man's ever been interested in me."

"Surely you're mistaken." Anna Weaver's soft voice was harder to hear. "He drove you all the way out here in the rain. That sure sounds to me like a fellow who wants to spend time with a girl."

"That was Susie's idea. At first, she wasn't so happy about the idea of a courtship with Eli, but now she seems to be trying to nudge things along. Not that it's done any good. He won't even talk to me. Making conversation with him is like pulling teeth."

Anna made a sympathetic noise. "He does seem like a quiet fellow. Maybe once you two know each other better, he'll start talking. I know! Mention the auction over at Owl Hollow. That would be a real fun outing, and Leah could go along as well."

"I did mention it. He's going, but he made it plain that he wants to go alone. It's the same as always, Anna." She gave a half-hearted laugh. "I don't know what's wrong with me, but fellows just aren't interested."

Wrong with her? He'd made Trudy think something was wrong with her?

Guiltily Eli shifted his weight from one boot to the other—and stepped right under a waterfall of cold rain spilling off the overhang. The water dripped off his hat and ran right down the back of his neck.

He shuddered. Was that why Trudy had brought up the Owl Hollow auction? Because she'd hoped he'd invite her to come along? The idea hadn't even occurred to him. He'd had his mind on those woodworking tools, so he'd only thought of it as a work trip.

And he'd not meant to be hard to talk to. He'd been worried, first over Leah's sickness and then that buggy wheel. He hadn't intended to hurt Trudy's feelings.

He had, though, and he hated it. Now he had one short buggy ride to make things right—and, as usual, no idea how to do it.

Trudy shivered and drew her shawl a little closer around herself as she stared over the sodden, dull fields. The ride home from Anna Weaver's store was even drearier than the ride over, but the unpleasant weather wasn't the only reason she was anxious for this trip to be over and done with.

Eli had seemed uncomfortable since he'd driven the buggy out onto the road. He was frowning, apparently lost in his own thoughts. He didn't look happy, and he hadn't said two words since they'd gotten back into the buggy.

Oh, he'd acted like he wanted to say something a time or two, but he hadn't—and she'd given up on trying to make conversation. If Eli didn't want to talk to her, fine. She'd let him alone, at least until they reached Susie's house.

But the minute they pulled in the driveway, she'd suggest they give up on this courtship idea. If this buggy ride was any indication, there was no hope of it going anywhere, anyway.

She'd felt so embarrassed at Anna's. Her friend had teased her gently about Eli driving her over, assuming this meant a courtship was afoot. It hadn't been much fun admitting that her new hopes had fizzled out so fast.

It hadn't been much fun admitting that to herself, either, but after this disaster of a buggy ride, she didn't see that she had much choice.

To be fair, he'd been real polite to her before they left. He'd insisted on carrying her bags, even though there wasn't that much to carry. Before today's drive, she might have taken that as a hopeful sign.

Now she knew better. Eli had carried her bags because he was a nice man. He'd have done the same for Anna or any other woman. It didn't mean he thought Trudy was special.

He must have only asked if she were interested in courting out of pity because he seemed to have little interest in talking to her or spending time with her. Even her hints about the Owl Hollow auction hadn't resulted in an invitation.

She sighed again. Well, it was a disappointment, but it wasn't the first one she'd had. She should never have gotten her hopes up in the first place.

Suddenly, Eli cleared his throat. "I was wondering. Did you have a chance to look at that board I left over at Susie's?"

Trudy wasn't sure exactly how she was supposed to answer that question. It was a board. Not much to look at. She still didn't see why Susie had been so interested in it. Which reminded her...

"Susie wanted me to ask you about that."

"What about it?"

The man was impossible, Trudy reflected with some exasperation. "I suppose she wanted to know why you brought it over and left it in her kitchen."

"Oh." His cheeks turned the color of bricks. "Well, you see, it's a piece of maple."

He'd said that before—although she had no idea why it should matter. "And?"

"A good piece. Really high-quality wood. It was left over from a hutch some *Englischers* special ordered to match a table they already had. Not many people want maple furniture any more. I don't see why," he went on. "It's a fine wood. Pretty and easy to work with. Sensible, too. It lasts well, maple does."

Trudy smothered another sigh. For the first time since they'd climbed into the buggy, Eli's expression had brightened.

Over a piece of wood.

"I see," she said politely—although she didn't. "Well, thank you. I'm sure it's a very nice board."

As they pulled into Susie's yard, Trudy drew a deep relieved breath. She'd best tell him now, while they were sitting in the yard, that they could drop this courtship idea. Surely, he wouldn't object.

It might make things a little uncomfortable with her babysitting Leah, Trudy reflected sadly, but that couldn't be helped. Anyway, she was fairly certain the only discomfort would be on her end. She doubted Eli would be the least bit bothered.

He was setting the brake, so it was time for her to speak. She clamped her fingers together and opened her mouth—but he spoke before she could.

"You know, we could go to that auction together, the one over in Owl Hollow. I should've asked you before. I just... I didn't think. But we could go together."

She was so surprised that she just sat for a second, staring at him.

"Unless," he added, "you'd rather not."

Trudy narrowed her eyes, studying him, trying to read

his face for clues. Had he overheard her conversation with Anna? He must have. He certainly hadn't been interested in taking her with him to the auction before.

She'd thought she couldn't feel any more embarrassed than she already did, but she'd been wrong. How much had he heard? She cast back in her mind, trying to remember what exactly she'd said.

"I wouldn't blame you if you didn't want to go," he went on. "I know I'm not... I'm not the best company. Never have been. I always say the wrong thing. Or do the wrong thing. Doesn't seem to matter how hard I try." He shot her an uneasy sideways glance. "What makes sense to me doesn't always make sense to other people. Like that board." He looked down at his boots, resting on the floorboard of the buggy. "I guess you think that was a *schtupid* thing, bringing you a board."

"Well." Trudy floundered for a tactful way to answer that question. "Maybe I just don't know enough about wood to understand what's special about it."

The red in his cheeks turned a shade darker. "It's the color of your hair."

She blinked. *"Vass?"*

"Or it will be once I'm done with it," he went on hurriedly, "Wood like that wants polishing to bring out its best. But with a little work and care, it'll be beautiful. Did you notice the grain? Those swirls will show up as different colors, just like the colors in your hair. There will be half a dozen shades of brown once I'm finished with it, and unless I miss my guess, it'll match just right."

"My hair." Her heart was pounding so hard she felt dizzy. Eli had noticed her hair? Eli thought her hair was...beautiful?

"Ja." He looked at her with surprise. "It's just the color

of maple, warm-like, with pretty light bits in it. That's why I thought... I thought I might make you something with that board, a keepsake, maybe. The trouble was, I couldn't figure what to make. I thought a box, maybe, for hairpins? I could make a *gut* one with a nice tight lid. But I wasn't sure you'd want that. Like I said, what makes sense to me doesn't make sense to other people. So I had the idea of bringing the board over for you to look at. Then, you could tell me straight out what you'd like to have."

"You want to make me a gift?" she asked softly.

"*Ja*. I don't know much about this courting business, but..." Another quick glance up at her face, then back down at his boots. "I figured...you know. It's sort of the thing a fellow might do for a woman he's taking buggy rides with."

Her heart suffused with a sweet, hopeful warmth. "That's very kind, Eli."

"I should have explained it better. But Leah was sick when I brought it over, and it always worries me, her getting sick. Once, not long after she came to me, she got a cold that turned into pneumonia. She ended up in the hospital for two days, and—" He stopped and swallowed hard. "It worries me when she gets sick," he repeated.

So that was why he'd been so distracted by a simple cold. Trudy felt a rush of sympathy.

"I'm sorry," she said. "I didn't understand."

"It's not your fault. A wooden board, even a good quality one, doesn't look like much to most people. But the beauty's there, all right. I see it, and I can bring it out. I'll take it home with me today and do my best to make you something worth keeping. Just tell me what you'd like."

"Anything," she said. "I'll be happy with anything you'd care to make for me. And *ja*, I'd like to go to the auction with you, Eli. *Denki* for asking."

"That's settled, then." Eli looked relieved. "Of course, I'll have to go to the wheelwright first." He offered her a quick half smile that made her heart stutter. "Else we might end up walking to that auction."

Trudy smiled. "Oh, I don't think I'd mind that so much."

Eli was in the act of stepping down from the buggy. He paused and looked at her, his expression skeptical.

"I expect you would. It's a fair step to Owl Hollow, and the weather's dicey this time of year."

"I meant," Trudy said, fighting a smile, "that I wouldn't mind walking *with you*."

"Ah." Eli had stepped out from under the shelter of the buggy. He stood there in the yard, rain pattering on his hat, looking up at her as if he couldn't quite believe what she'd said. "Well, then. That's a…that's a real fine thing for a fellow to hear. But I'm still going to see the wheelwright. You wait there, and I'll help you down. Everything's slick. Take the umbrella and stop fussing with those packages. I'll bring them along."

He spoke brusquely, but she noticed as he rounded the buggy, that Eli was fighting a smile of his own.

Chapter Eight

Eli snapped the reins on Star's back, listening to Trudy and Leah's cheerful chatter. They'd been talking ever since he'd picked Trudy up just after dawn. He'd have thought that since the two spent almost every day together, they'd have run out of things to talk about.

He was thankful that wasn't the case. Leah tended to get *naerfich* when there was a lot of traffic on the road, and they weren't the only people headed to the auction. This normally quiet country road was busy today. Cars passed them regularly, and he was glad that talking to Trudy had Leah so nicely distracted.

Their conversation ranged from the beautiful weather on this crisp fall day, to the pretty farms and fields rolling by, to what Leah would choose for lunch from the food stalls at the auction. Now Leah wanted to know what Trudy might buy if she had all the money in the world.

"I don't know," Trudy said thoughtfully. "A house, I suppose. It would be real nice to have a home of my own." She caught Eli's eye and flushed a pretty pink. "Of course, I'm not likely to ever have all the money in the world, so I don't suppose it matters."

"We don't have our own house anymore," Leah announced sadly. "We used to, but now we just live in our *kossin* Vernon's backyard." She wrinkled her nose.

"And we're thankful," Eli reminded his niece. "Thankful to have a nice place to live so close to our family and my work while we're getting started here. Our *kossins* have been very generous. Our home is a blessing from *Gott,* and we don't complain."

"I know," Leah said with a solemn nod. "I'm sorry. I'm thankful. I'd just be more thankful if we didn't live so close to *kossin* Jane."

Trudy smothered a giggle, and Eli shot her an agonized look, hoping she'd change the subject. He didn't blame Leah for feeling as she did. Jane could be stern, and she was real particular about her garden and yard. But they'd both have to put up with her fussing until they had a place of their own.

Which, he supposed, might be something he should start looking into. He glanced over at Trudy.

She was looking extra pretty today. She had on a dark green dress that suited her real well, and she'd hardly stopped smiling since she'd climbed in the buggy.

He liked it when she smiled.

"Well, I don't expect you'll be living there forever," Trudy was saying. "In the meantime, you'll just have to be patient. Try counting up the things you like about where you're living now rather than the things you don't."

"Well," Leah considered, "I like playing with the barn cats. The gray cat just had kittens, and—"

Just then two cars passed their buggy in a rush of smelly air. The smaller car revved its engine as it went by, the *Englischers* gawking and pointing.

The gelding flicked an uneasy ear but stayed his course. He was too experienced a buggy horse to overreact to cars.

But Leah laid her hand on Eli's forearm and clamped down tight, the beloved new kittens temporarily forgotten.

"Are we almost there?" she whispered.

"Almost," he said.

"You're going to have such fun at the auction, Leah," Trudy promised cheerfully.

"Looking at tools?" Leah didn't sound convinced. "That's what *Onkel* says we're going to do."

"There's all sorts of other things to look at, too. And just about all our friends from Hickory Springs will be there. Wait and see. You're going to have a real *gut* time."

Eli wasn't so sure. This particular auction was likely to be an extra busy one. Leah had never been in a crowd that size, and he wasn't sure how well she'd handle it.

When the auction site came into view, his worries multiplied like the Flauds' barn cats. The event was being held at a local farm, and the place was buzzing like an overturned beehive. Eli drove Star in the direction of the neatly lined up black buggies, positioned along a fence that could be used as a makeshift hitching post. The row of buggies seemed endless, and there were cars parked along the roadway as far as he could see.

"So many people," Leah murmured shakily, her eyes wide.

"Ja," Trudy said brightly as she adjusted Leah's bonnet. "Isn't it wonderful? This auction is to raise money for a very sick little boy. He was in an accident and needs lots of care to get better. Our two communities have come together to do this auction so that the family can pay for all his doctor bills. The more folks, the more money, so this crowd is a wonderful *gut* thing to see!"

"Oh." Leah considered this. "Can we buy some things to help the little boy, too?" She sniffed. The air was rich with the scent of fried pies, popcorn and roasting meat. "Maybe something to eat?"

Trudy laughed. "We'll start with that. If," she added, "your *onkel* doesn't mind."

"As soon as I get registered for the bidding, we'll find some food," he promised.

The line to register was lengthy, and it took a while to get his number. Once he had that safely in hand, they followed their noses to the food stalls. There was plenty to choose from. The women of Owl Hollow and Hickory Springs had gone all out. Table after table boasted delicious goodies: candy, cookies, fried pies, individual slices of cake, and bags of popcorn and nuts.

Leah had never been offered so many choices. She held tightly to Trudy's hand and peered with interest at all the tempting offerings. But as they inspected table after table, Eli noticed the little girl growing agitated.

"So?" Trudy asked when they had made their way slowly down the long row of tables. "Have you decided what snack you want?"

"I don't know!" Leah wailed. "There's too many things to pick from, and I'm hungry right now. I don't know what to do!"

Eli's stomach twisted into a knot. This was what he'd worried about, that the crowd and noise of a big auction would be too much for Leah. That she'd get overwhelmed and have a meltdown. He'd really have liked a look at the tools, but he didn't want Leah upset. Probably best just to give up and go home.

Before he could suggest that, Trudy laughed.

"I know! There's so much that I'm having trouble deciding myself. But that's all right. See? That booth over there is offering samples of their candy for a donation. Let's go over and get a few bites to tide us over. Then we'll walk through again. You can take your time and pick out just what you'd most like to eat."

As Leah thought that suggestion over, her finger came out of her mouth, which Eli took as a good sign.

"All right," she agreed, and they headed over to the table offering candy samples.

Eli followed, shaking his head in silent admiration. Somehow Trudy always knew just the right thing to do or say.

On the other hand, another pass through the food tables would take a while. He glanced toward the big barn where the tools were arranged for folks to view before the bidding started. He needed to examine the tools so that he could decide on his top bids ahead of time. Leah wasn't the only one who got flustered in a crowd, and he couldn't afford to make a mistake and overpay for a tool that was damaged.

"Go ahead."

Startled out of his thoughts, he looked back at Trudy. "What?"

"Go ahead and look over the tools. That's what you've come for, ain't so?"

"Well, *ja*. That and—" *To spend time with you, like I'm supposed to.* He wasn't sure exactly how to put that. "Shouldn't we stay together?"

"Probably better you go alone, so you can check everything over without being distracted. Leah and I will figure out what snack we want, and then we'll find a place to eat."

He hesitated, looking down at Leah, who was pointing at a small piece of divinity candy. "It's a big crowd," he muttered uneasily.

"You'll be near the woodworking tools, won't you?" Trudy handed over a quarter to the Owl Creek woman with a smile and gave Leah the piece of candy. "You shouldn't be so hard to find if we need you for anything. Don't worry about us. We're having fun, aren't we, Leah?"

The child nodded as she chewed. *"Ja,"* she managed stickily. "Fun."

Trudy laughed and tapped the child's nose playfully. "You'd best hurry," she told Eli. "It looks like the bidding's going to start soon."

He frowned. For a woman who'd wanted a courtship, she sure seemed anxious to be rid of him.

"All right." Quickly he counted out money and pressed it into Trudy's hand. "Buy treats for both of you," he told her. "And…"

He trailed off. He wanted to say, *And be careful*. The crowd really was large, with lots of *Englischers* mingled among the Plain folks.

He knew most *Englischers* were nice people. He'd met plenty of them. But some weren't, like the teenagers Abby had fallen in with. Before Abby had jumped the fence, he'd not given much thought to *Englischers*. They lived outside his world. They were customers and drivers and sometimes employers, but that was all.

Now, though, he knew what trouble and heartache the wrong sort of *Englischers* could cause if you let them get too close.

Trudy was watching him. She'd tucked the money he'd handed her in her bag and now she held a piece of divinity in her fingers, one small bite missing. As he fumbled for words, a spark of understanding lit her eyes.

"We will be all right, Eli," she said. "If we have any trouble finding you after the bidding's over, we'll just go out and wait in the buggy. I remember right where we left it."

"Gut." He liked that they had a plan. "See you in a little while. Okay, Leah?"

"Okay." She tugged Trudy's hand. "Can we go look again? I think maybe I want to have one of those peach pies with the white frosting on the top, but I'm not sure."

"I think that would be a very good choice. Let's go take another look." Trudy glanced up at Eli, smiling her big generous smile. She gave him a little wave with her free hand. "I hope you get a good deal on the tools you want."

He hesitated, watching them walk away. Suddenly, he wasn't so interested in tools at all. He'd rather have wandered among the food stalls with Trudy and Leah—but it was pretty clear he wasn't invited.

Nursing some slightly bruised feelings, he started toward the auction area, which was already packed with men interested in the various items going on the block. He had no trouble finding the woodworking tools, which were laid out neatly for inspection.

He leaned over, carefully examining chisels, clamps, gouges and sharpening stones. It was a big collection, all roughly of the same vintage and good quality.

He picked up a marking gauge, running his hand over the wooden beam. A good piece, not new, but well made. He could use something like this, and it was in a batch with some nice chisels.

"Those are good tools." A Plain man, roughly his age, was standing beside him, looking down at the table. "And they've been well looked after. They'll outlast any man that buys them."

Eli nodded. "That's true. You don't often see such tools up for sale at an auction. Somebody didn't know what they had."

"Oh, we knew." When Eli shot him a surprised look, the man went on. "Those were my *grossdaddi*'s tools. He only bought quality, and he tended them like they were his children."

"I'd think such tools would be kept in the family."

"None of us have any skill at woodworking, so it seems selfish to keep them when the Stoll family needs money for their boy's medical expenses. I only spoke up because I wanted you to know that you'd be getting your money's worth if you win the bidding."

Eli started to say he'd enough sense to see that for himself but thought better of it. "Well, if I do end up with them, you can rest easy knowing I'll keep them well, just as your *grossdaddi* did."

For once in his life, Eli seemed to have said the right thing because the man smiled. "That would please him. They'll serve you well if you do, you and your sons after you. I hope you win the bid."

As the stranger turned to shoulder his way through the crowd, Eli stood frozen, the tools forgotten.

His sons.

He'd never thought much about having sons of his own. There wasn't much point in a man thinking about things—in wanting things—that he wasn't likely to have.

He glanced toward the field where people were milling thickly around the sales stalls. He couldn't see Trudy, but no doubt she was there, patiently leading Leah from table to table. By herself, so that he could take his time looking over these tools, even though this outing was supposed to be an opportunity for them to spend time together and get to know each other.

He wasn't sure how much she'd learned about him so far, but he'd learned plenty about her. He'd learned that she was cheerful. She was kind and unselfish. And, of course, she had a real knack with children.

He'd learned something about himself today, too. Something surprising.

He'd like to have sons. More daughters, too, if *Gott* willed it. In fact, he'd like a big family, one so large that there was a crowd around the dinner table every night.

He could see them in his mind's eye, clear as day, the *kinder*. Leah the oldest, a few sturdy little boys sprinkled with sawdust from learning beside him in his workshop, and then more children, like stairsteps, ranging down to a babe in arms.

All of them happy. All of them his, to love and look after. And all of them with smiles just a little too big for their faces.

Maybe, he realized, just maybe, he didn't want this courtship to fizzle out. Maybe he wanted…more.

He felt winded, like a mule had just kicked him in the belly. He was still trying to gather his wits when a man walked up and began loading the tools onto a wagon.

"These lots are up next," he told Eli. "If you want to bid, best go take your place."

"Denki." Eli blinked and started toward the crowd where the auctioneer's banter was lilting from a makeshift platform, his determination growing with every step.

Ja, he wanted to bid, and he'd pay whatever he had to.

He suddenly wanted those tools more than he'd ever wanted anything in his life.

Trudy and Leah sat on the seat of Eli's buggy, eating their fried pies and drinking cold sodas. There'd been no place to sit near the sales tables, and they'd not thought to bring an old quilt to spread on the ground, so Trudy had suggested they eat in the buggy.

Relieved to be in the happy solitude of her *onkel*'s buggy,

Leah was enjoying her pie, licking her fingers enthusiastically after each bite. Trudy nibbled hers slowly, watching the people and straining her ears to hear the low cadence of the auctioneer's voice.

She hadn't been in such a big crowd since her *kossin*'s wedding, and she'd enjoyed the energy and the happy camaraderie. She would've liked to spend more time bumping elbows with all the people and browsing through all the interesting items the two communities had donated for auction.

However, probably by the time Leah was finished with her snack, Eli would be ready to go home. He obviously didn't like crowds any more than Leah did.

Trudy watched as a Plain family—parents and four small children—walked past the buggy on the way toward the big barn, smiling and talking to each other in *Deutsch.*

Attending an auction made a fun change for the adults, a little break from the endless chores at home. The children would likely enjoy the treats and the commotion. No doubt the little ones would sleep well tonight, exhausted by the excitement of their outing. And the parents would sit together by lamplight talking over their day.

Trudy sighed wistfully, and Leah looked up, her lips smeared with white sugar icing.

"What's wrong?" she asked around a mouthful.

Trudy smiled—and dodged the question. "Chew and swallow before you talk," she instructed in her best nanny voice. As she reached out with a paper napkin to dab the child's face clean, she saw Eli walking down the slope from the barn. He had a large canvas bag slung over one shoulder. "Here comes your *onkel*. Looks like you got the tools!" she called when he came within earshot.

"I did."

He must have gotten a good bargain, too, Trudy, thought, going by the smile on his face.

He walked to the rear of the buggy to stow the tools in the chest strapped there. When he reappeared, Trudy reached over to gather the napkin and scrap of uneaten pie out of Leah's lap.

"I'll hold this while you climb in the back," she told the little girl. "You can finish eating on the ride home."

"You don't want to leave already, do you?" Eli asked.

Trudy looked at him with surprise. "You want to stay longer? Is there something else you'd like to bid on?"

He shook his head. "I've got what I came after. I thought maybe you'd like to see what all they have. They've got a good many quilts up for bidding and some home furnishings. But if you'd rather go—"

"*Nee*! I'm in no hurry at all. And I'd love to see the quilts!" She quickly wrapped up the remaining scraps of their snacks and started to climb out of the buggy.

She was careless in her hurry, and her fingers were a little oily from the fried pie, and she slipped. Immediately, Eli caught her elbow, steadying her.

Startled, she glanced up at him.

"Careful," was all he said. But as their eyes met, she thought she saw a glimmer of something new in his. That little glint—combined with the strong warmth of his fingers—made her stomach do somersaults.

"Help me," Leah demanded. Eli turned away and reached up to help his niece. When he looked back at Trudy, he seemed just the same as always.

"We'd best hurry," he said. "The auction's moving fast and there won't be much left to see if we don't."

They wandered through the barns and outbuildings, examining the items for sale. Eli didn't talk much, but now and then Trudy nudged him for an opinion. She was curious to see if they shared the same tastes and—largely—they did.

Sometimes, though, Eli surprised her.

As they walked past a mixed lot of odds and ends, he stopped to inspect an old rocker. He glanced at her. "What do you think of this?"

She hesitated. The chair looked awfully battered and dingy. "I suppose it was nice once, but it's ruined now."

"It's not." Eli ran a practiced hand over the wood. "This chair was well made by a man who knew his business, so even though it's old and has seen hard use, it's still sound. See?" He flipped it upside down and waggled the legs attached to the curved rocker. "They hardly move. It just needs a good stripping and repolishing, and this spindle here would have to be sanded smooth. Looks like it got chewed on. Probably stored in somebody's barn. Cleaned up, this chair would be real comfortable and nice to look at."

"Do you want to bid on it?"

Eli laughed shortly. He had a nice laugh, she thought, although she'd hardly ever heard it. "*Nee*. I can make something just as nice. It's a pity, though. Some fellow like me put a lot of time into this. I hate to see it in such sad condition when it might've lasted another hundred years. Speaking of time." He pulled out his pocket watch. "They'll start auctioning off the quilts around three, so we'd better go look them over if you'd still like to."

Before Trudy could answer, a young *Englisch* man stepped close and cleared his throat. A pretty woman, obviously in the last stages of a pregnancy, hovered behind him.

"Sorry to bother you," the man said. "But could I ask you a question?"

Trudy smiled at him. "Of course."

"I don't know much about furniture." He looked hopefully at Eli. "We want a rocking chair for the nursery, and I figured this one might go cheap, but it looks pretty rough. I saw you checking it out. Do you think it could be fixed?"

Still smiling, Trudy glanced at Eli. He was studying the young couple with a frown—and, to her mind, taking an awful long time to answer.

"Eli makes furniture for a living," she volunteered. "And he was just saying what a good piece this was. Weren't you?"

"*Ja*, it's a good piece for somebody willing to put some work into it." Eli answered shortly—and in *Deutsch,* so there was no way the young man could understand.

Trudy shot him a surprised, reproachful look before turning back to the *Englischer.* "He says it'll take some work," she translated politely. "But it was well made, so *ja*, it can be fixed."

"We have to go now." Eli spoke in English, clearly and decisively. Leaning over he swept Leah up in his arms. "Come on, Trudy," he said, reverting to *Deutsch.* "Let's go look at the quilts."

Trudy flashed an apologetic smile at the young couple. "I'm sorry. We have to go. I hope you get the chair!"

She hurried after Eli. He slowed, allowing her to catch up, but he didn't stop walking until they were a good distance away.

"Were those bad people?" Leah had stuck her finger back into her mouth, and her eyes were wide.

"*Nee*, they were very friendly and very polite," Trudy assured her.

"They were *Englisch*," Eli said flatly. "They aren't like us. The less we have to do with such folks, the better."

They walked inside a big shed where quilts were hanging on rods, displayed for potential buyers before going up for bidding. There were dozens, all shapes and sizes, each one prettier than the last—but Trudy had a hard time focusing on them.

She'd never seen Eli be impolite before. He could be thoughtless sometimes, but that seemed accidental. With the *Englisch* couple, though, he'd been pretty rude—and she wondered why.

She glanced at him and found him looking back.

"Take your time and look all you like," he said gruffly. "And if you want to stay to watch the bidding, I'll find us a spot where you can see and hear everything."

"*Nee*, I only wanted to look them over. It won't take long, but you can wait outside if you'd rather. I'm sure you're not so interested in quilts."

Eli scanned the crowd and shook his head. "A lot of people in here, all sorts. Best we stay together."

His uneasiness was catching. Leah kept her finger in her mouth and grasped Trudy's skirt tightly with her other hand.

Trudy paused in front of a quilt with a large navy star in its middle. It was a bold quilt with strong lines, and she knew right away who'd donated it. Only Lilah Miller, the local shopkeeper's wife, quilted with such intense colors, and her quilts were always showstoppers. Now that she had a growing family to look after, her quilts were harder to come by, so likely this one would bring a high price.

A burst of laughter came from a group of *Englischers* standing nearby. Leah huddled closer and whispered, "Are those people laughing at us?"

Trudy stooped and cupped the girl's chin in her palm, holding the child's worried gaze with her own.

"*Nee*, of course not. They're laughing because they're happy. The money made here is for little Andy Stoll. Like I told you, he's been very sick, and we all—Plain folks and *Englischers* both—are thankful we've found a way to help him and his family. Those people are laughing because that's the best kind of happiness there is—the kind we feel when we help someone else."

Leah's expression relaxed. "I'm thankful, too. Maybe I could give the sick boy one of the new barn kittens. That might make him feel better." She yawned and scrubbed at her eyes.

"Somebody's tired," Trudy murmured to Eli.

He was watching her with a funny expression on his face. But all he said was, "I can carry her, if you want to keep looking."

"I've seen enough."

Eli nodded, and when Leah yawned again, he leaned over and gathered his niece up in his arms. "All right, then. Let's go."

By the time they reached the buggy, Leah's eyelids were drooping, so Eli settled her in the back seat, padding her carefully with a thick blanket and using a smaller lap blanket for a pillow. Leah smiled at him sleepily, then snuggled up and closed her eyes.

The parking area was thick with people, but Eli was a deft driver and Star a well-trained horse, so it wasn't long before they were on the road homeward.

"I'm glad you got the tools you wanted," Trudy said.

"Me, too. They'll—" he started, then stopped short. "They'll last me a lifetime," he finished, but she had an odd feeling that wasn't what he'd started to say. "Thanks for taking charge of Leah while I was bidding."

"I didn't mind. I think Leah had a nice time, except for being a little *naerfich*." She hesitated but decided to speak honestly. "I think you scared her some, being so unfriendly to that young couple."

Eli didn't take his eyes off the road. He shrugged. "If

she's scared of *Englischers*, it'll suit me fine. I don't want her having anything to do with them." He flicked the reins on Star's back.

"But those people weren't bothering us. The man just wanted to buy his wife a chair for their baby's nursery."

"Any grown man should know a good piece of furniture when he sees it without asking. And we don't know that woman was his wife. Just as likely not, the way *Englisch* men are. They'll get a girl—" he stopped short "—in a fix," he continued carefully, "and then run off and not even have the decency to be ashamed of themselves."

The bitterness in his voice stunned Trudy into silence. Forgiveness and a gentle tolerance for the shortcomings of others was drilled into Plain children from birth. Why would Eli say such things? Unless...

You need to ask more questions, Trudy. Susie's advice echoed sharply in her memory.

She glanced cautiously over her shoulder. Leah appeared sound asleep, but Trudy kept her voice low.

"Eli? Are you angry because...because that's what happened to your sister?"

Eli didn't answer right away, and the longer the silence stretched, the more Trudy regretted asking the question.

"I'm sorry," she said finally. "I didn't mean to pry."

He cut her a quick sideways glance. "That's all right. I don't go out of my way to talk about Abby's troubles to everybody, but you...you have a right to know. Or at least..." A muscle twitched in his cheek. "To know as much as I do, which isn't much. I'm not even sure Abby's still alive. She was heading down a dangerous road, last time I saw her. That was two years ago, the day she left Leah with me." He kept his eyes on the road ahead. "It was the first I'd seen of her since the night she ran off with those *Englisch* friends of hers."

The pain in his voice made Trudy wince. She shouldn't have brought this up. "You don't have to talk about this if you don't want to, Eli."

He sighed. "You might as well hear the whole story. It's not a pretty one. My *mamm* and *daed* died in a buggy accident when I was a teenager. Abby's younger than me, and I wasn't old enough yet to look after her, so we went to live with an *aent* and *onkel*. They fed us and clothed us, but they weren't…" His expression went a shade grimmer. "They weren't the easiest people to live with. My *onkel* was raised in a strict community, and he still held those ways of thinking and doing things. And my *aent*, she never had any children of her own, and she didn't seem to know how to be a mother. Maybe if she'd been more like you, Abby wouldn't have run off like she did."

More like you. Trudy battled a guilty swell of pleasure at Eli's words. It was wrong to compare people. *Gott* in His wisdom gave each person different abilities, and whatever gifts a person received were to be used for the benefit of the whole community. She certainly shouldn't feel proud that Eli thought she was better with children than his *aent*.

But she couldn't help but feel a little bit thankful that he did.

"The stricter they tried to be, the worse Abby got. She ran wild with *Englisch* boys. Sneaked out at night. Started drinking." His cheeks flushed. "And then left home and had a baby without getting married."

Abby had also broken her brother's heart. Eli didn't have to tell her that. It was written all over his face.

"And you've not heard anything from her since she left Leah with you?"

"Not a word. There's a post office box. She wrote down that number for me, and I've written her letters. She's never answered. That's likely my fault. We...argued that last day." He threw Trudy a guilty look. "I told her she couldn't leave Leah with me. I didn't know anything about taking care of a little girl..."

"But you changed your mind."

"I didn't have much choice. Abby wasn't in any shape to take care of a little one." The muscle twitched in his cheek again. "Once I understood how bad off she was, I told her I'd take Leah. But that's not all I told her. I said other things, too, things I shouldn't have said. Hard things."

"True things."

"What?" He glanced at her as if she'd startled him.

"I think you're being very unkind to yourself." She laid a hand on his forearm, and his muscle tensed beneath her fingers. "Maybe you did speak a little too plainly to Abby that day. I don't know. But I know this. Whatever you said to your sister, it was the truth. You wouldn't say anything to her—or to me or to anybody else—that wasn't true. You're the most honest man I've ever met."

It was a good thing that Star was a well-trained horse because Eli seemed to have forgotten he was driving a buggy. He stared at her for a long moment, the reins gone slack in his fingers.

Then his expression shuttered, and he turned his attention back to the road. "I wouldn't be so sure of that," he muttered.

And she could barely get another word out of him for the rest of the drive back to Susie's.

Chapter Nine

From her seat at Susie's kitchen table, Trudy's mother, Vera Schwartz, watched as Leah sat in the living room, coloring a picture of a farmyard with crayons.

"Well, for sure and certain she's a neat, well-behaved child," *Mamm* murmured. She lifted her steaming cup of tea and took a cautious sip. "I didn't know what to expect of a girl being brought up with only an *onkel* looking after her."

The curiosity in her mother's eyes made Trudy stir her tea a little faster. It looked like *Mamm* was finally getting to the point of this unexpected visit.

She'd claimed she'd come by to drop off a coat and a thick shawl Trudy had left behind. The weather had taken a turn during the past week, and the temperatures had dipped, so that made sense. But Trudy suspected *Mamm*'s real purpose was to find out if her daughter and the newcomer Eli Mast were—as the Hickory Springs gossip suggested—becoming a couple.

"Eli takes very good care of Leah." Trudy kept her voice carefully neutral, but her mother pounced like a cat with a ball of yarn.

"*Ja*, I've been hearing how highly you think of him." Her *mamm*'s brown eyes twinkled over the rim of her teacup. "I hear he thinks pretty well of you, too."

Instead of answering, Trudy raised her own cup to her mouth so fast that she sloshed tea over the rim.

She wasn't prepared for this conversation today. Apparently *Mamm* was here to figure out how likely it was that she'd be planning a wedding next year, and Trudy didn't know the answer. The small amount of time she'd spent with Eli so far had left her with jumbled feelings, and she hadn't been able to make much sense of them yet.

On the one hand, the gossips were right. She did think highly of him. Eli Mast was a hardworking, decent man with a *gut* heart. His patience with Leah was remarkable. Many Plain fathers, busy with the hard work required to support their rapidly growing families, might have grown impatient with a *naerfich* child like Leah. But Eli never had, and she liked that about him—very much.

There was something else she liked about him, too, something more selfish. She'd really liked that comment he'd made about the maple wood reminding him of her hair. No fellow had ever marked Trudy's hair—nor anything else about her—as special before. Not once.

He wasn't perfect. Eli was awkward, and sometimes he said things the wrong way. He didn't mean to be hurtful, but sometimes the clumsy things he said stung—partly because you knew he was speaking honestly.

That was another thing. She'd been troubled by that remark he'd made on their way home from the auction—about not being so honest as she thought he was.

She wondered what he'd meant by that—and if it had anything to do with why Susie had been unwilling to set up a match for him the day he'd come to see her.

"Are you going to drink that whole cup of tea before answering me?" Her mother lifted her eyebrows. "I'd figured you'd be bubbling over. In fact, I've been expecting you to stop by the house to tell us all about this man. If you're worried about the child overhearing, I don't think she's listening to us at all."

Trudy set her teacup back into its saucer. "There's not much to tell, *Mamm*."

Mamm threw her a skeptical look. "The rest of Hickory Springs would disagree. Folks have been talking plenty, and everybody's real happy for you."

"That's nice," Trudy tried desperately to come up with a way to change the subject. Why had she ever thought it would be fun to be the focus of Hickory Springs' courtship gossip? "Have Hannah and Andy set their moving day yet?" Her second oldest sister and brother-in-law had recently purchased a new home, and the family had been waiting to hear when the move would be scheduled.

Her mother nodded. "It's to be next Saturday, and we've decided to make a family frolic out of it. Your father and I talked it over, and we'd like you to bring Eli." She smiled, a triumphant twinkle in her eye. "That way we can all get to know him."

"Oh!" Trudy felt like a firefly caught in a mason jar. Desperately, she looked for some way to wriggle out of this plan. Introduce crowd-hating Eli to her six siblings and their families, plus her parents, all at once? "I'm not sure that's a good idea…"

"I don't see why not. Your sisters' special friends always came and pitched in when there was family work to be done, didn't they?"

"But they knew everybody already, *Mamm*. They'd all grown up here, so they were comfortable with us. Eli's new to Hickory Springs."

"All the more reason to invite him." *Mamm* made an impatient noise. "Of course, I'm assuming he needs to get comfortable with our family. Trudy, I'm just going to come right out and ask. Do you consider this Eli Mast a special friend—the kind of friend your family should meet and get to know—or not?"

There was no dodging that question. Trudy swallowed hard. "There's nothing for sure, *Mamm*. But I think—he might be."

"Well, then!" Beaming, *Mamm* sat back in her chair. "Naturally, he'll expect to spend time with your family, and we might as well start now. It's always best to begin as you plan to go on. We'll see you both at the work frolic."

Trudy sighed—and surrendered. "All right. I'll talk to Eli and see what he says."

"I'm sure he'll be happy to come."

Trudy wasn't so sure of that at all, so she stayed silent. Flushed with her success, *Mamm* carried her cup and saucer to the sink to rinse. Then she walked into the living room where Leah knelt in front of a low table, coloring a duck's bill orange.

The child looked up, her expression uncertain. *Mamm* smiled warmly.

"You've been very quiet so that Trudy and I could talk. And—" the older woman craned her neck to see the picture Leah was working on "—you've colored that page very neatly. Here." Vera pulled a small candy bar out of her bag and placed it beside the box of crayons on the table. "A treat for behaving so well. You like chocolate, don't you?"

Surprised, Leah nodded.

"I figured so. All my other grandchildren do, too, so I make sure I have plenty in my bag for whenever I catch them behaving well and working hard."

All my other grandchildren. Trudy caught her breath sharply.

"*Denki-shay,*" Leah murmured politely, picking up the candy.

"*Du bisht welcome*, Leah. And you can call me *Mammi* Vera, just as the others do."

"*Denki, Mammi* Vera."

Vera nodded, then turned and brushed past Trudy into the kitchen. She placed her black bonnet over her *kapp* and tied it with firm decisive twists.

"That was kind of you, *Mamm*," Trudy said around the knot that had formed in her throat. "But Eli and I haven't... We aren't—"

"Not yet maybe," her mother interrupted with a shrug. "But it seems to be headed that way. And like I said—always best to begin as you plan to go on. Now, I'll expect to see you and Eli on Saturday. Bring the child with you. She needs to get to know everybody, too."

With that, *Mamm* bustled out into the chilly autumn sunshine.

Trudy fretted over her mother's invitation for the rest of the afternoon. She went back and forth between being deeply touched by *Mamm*'s unconditional acceptance of Leah as a potential granddaughter and concerned about how Eli would feel about being steamrolled into meeting her big noisy family—all of them at once.

At half past five o'clock, when Trudy walked to the back door for the tenth time—she thought she'd heard a buggy—Susie sighed. She'd come home from the bakery eager to try a new bread dough recipe, and she'd enlisted Leah's help with the mixing.

"You know what they say about watched pots, Trudy."

"I know. I just... I need to ask Eli about something when he gets here. I hoped to meet him in the yard." She'd prefer to have this conversation in private.

"Well, it's a nice day out. Why don't the two of you take a walk and talk over whatever you need to? Leah and I have our hands full getting these rolls shaped and ready to for their second rise, don't we?"

"*Ja*! I love baking with you, Susie!" Leah happily rolled the ball of dough she'd been given on the floured surface of the table.

Susie caught the child in a warm one-armed hug. "I love baking with you, too."

Movement outside caught Trudy's eye, and she turned to see Eli's buggy pulling into the yard. "All right, then. I'll leave you two to your work and see if I can talk Eli into a quick walk around Miller's pond."

Trudy threw the shawl her mother had brought over her shoulders—the sun was bright, but the afternoon air had the bite of mid-fall—and stepped outside onto the back stoop. Eli was just setting the brake on the buggy. He glanced up and smiled.

Trudy's heart did a quick thump and bump in her chest. When he smiled like that, Eli was a very nice-looking fellow.

He jumped out of the buggy and started halfway across the yard. He had a sprinkling of sawdust on his sleeves, she noticed, and when he drew nearer, she caught the scent of newly sawed wood.

"What are you doing standing out here in the chill?" His smile faded. "Is something wrong with Leah?"

"*Nee*, she's fine. I'd like to talk to you about something. Susie said she'd keep an eye on Leah so we could take a walk."

Eli hesitated. "All right," he said after a long reluctant pause.

"You don't look too happy," Trudy said. She brushed a

drift of sawdust off his sleeve. "You've been working hard today, I see. Are you too tired to walk around a little?"

"*Nee*. I'm not so tired, and I like walking." In spite of his words, his face had a grim set to it. "Where do you want to go?"

"I thought we'd walk around Ephraim Miller's pond." Trudy pointed to the small circular pond in the field behind Susie's house. "He doesn't mind. He tells Susie to fish in it all she wants, and we even waded in it some this past summer when the days got hot."

"All right."

They walked in silence for a few minutes, Trudy sneaking quick worried glances at him every few steps. His face was set in tight resigned lines; his earlier smile was nowhere to be seen—and he wasn't saying a word.

"Is it me, Eli?" she blurted out.

"Is what you?"

"Well, you're not tired, and you say you like walking, but you look as gloomy as a thundercloud and you're awfully quiet. Is it spending time with me you're not so happy about?"

He stopped short. "*Nee*, Trudy." He spoke so sincerely that she believed him. "It's not you. It's…"

He left the sentence dangling so long that finally she prompted, "It's what?"

"The talking. I'm not so *gut* at the talking. I'm always saying something I shouldn't, or—" he cut her a sharp, worried glance. "Or I'm not saying something I should."

Trudy felt so relieved that she laughed. "Don't worry about that, Eli. If you say the wrong thing, we'll just back up and start over. All right?"

He looked down at her, and his expression softened. "All

right." As they started walking again, he added, "What do you need to talk to me about? Something about Leah?"

"*Nee*, it's about my family. My mother stopped by today. They're having a work frolic at my sister Hannah's new home, and they wanted me to invite you." Briefly, she explained about her sister and brother-in-law Andy Chupp's move and how the Schwartz family was planning to help get them settled in the following Saturday.

"Oh." Eli appeared to think this over. "Is there something there they need my help with? Woodwork or cabinetry or something like that?"

"*Nee*, not that I know of. They just want to meet you."

They'd reached the pond now, and Eli stopped. He looked over the sparkling water, ruffled by the brisk October breeze. Trees fringed the pond and were reflected in it, their leaves just now beginning to show the warm colors of autumn.

"It's so pretty here," Trudy murmured.

"Why?"

She glanced up at Eli, startled.

"Well, I don't know," she floundered. "I just think it's pretty. Don't you? You know, the sun on the water, and the yellow and orange leaves, and—"

"*Nee.*" For the first time since they'd left Susie's yard, a tiny smile lifted one corner of Eli's mouth. "I wasn't talking about the pond, Trudy. I meant why does your family want to meet me?"

She tried to think of a good way to state what surely he should know without being told. "*Mamm* heard... You know, people in Hickory Springs have noticed that we..." She trailed off, watching his face for signs that he knew what she was getting at and hoping he'd speak up and save her from having to say it straight out.

But Eli said nothing, so finally Trudy sighed and put her fists on her hips.

"We're courting, Eli! Or we're supposed to be. Naturally, my family's excited and they want to get to know you and Leah." Trudy hesitated. "I guess I should tell you, my *mamm* has already asked Leah to call her *Mammi* Vera. That's what her other...her grandchildren all call her. I hope you don't mind. She means well."

"She did that?" Eli didn't look annoyed at all, Trudy noticed with some relief. He only looked thoughtful. And maybe—she thought—a little bit pleased.

"*Ja*, and in the interest of full honesty, I should warn you *Mamm* will sneak her chocolate every chance she gets."

He thought it over for a moment, frowning. "I'll come to the frolic." He made the announcement with a dogged determination.

"There's a lot of us," she warned. "It'll be a crowd."

Eli's expression didn't change. "I'll come," he repeated. "And if they do need any woodworking help on the new house, tell them I'll be bringing my tools."

Trudy felt a rush of relief. "That's very kind of you, Eli. My *mamm* will be so pleased."

He glanced down at her. "I appreciate your *mamm* being *freindlich* to Leah, but I'm not going to the frolic because it'll please her. I'm going because it'll please you."

"Oh!" Trudy was so surprised that for a second she had no idea what to say. "Well, *denki-shay*, Eli," she said at last, offering a shy smile.

His eyes dropped to her mouth and lingered. "I like to see you smile," he said gruffly. Then his cheeks went red, and he quickly looked away. "Now, if that's all you wanted to talk about, we'd best get back. Leah will be wanting her supper."

He turned and started back toward Susie's, pausing long

enough for her to catch up with him. They walked side by side in silence until they reached Susie's kitchen.

But this time, Trudy didn't mind so much.

On the Saturday of the work frolic, Eli adjusted the tool belt he wore around his waist and opened one of the cabinets in Andy and Hannah Chupp's kitchen, testing the hinge—and wishing there was room for him to climb into it and hide.

Trudy's sister and brother-in-law were nice people. In fact, the whole family had been nothing but friendly to him since he had driven Trudy and Leah over early that morning.

There were just so many of them.

A man couldn't take two steps in any direction without stumbling over three or four people. The Schwartz family and their spouses filled the Chupps' smallish house to overflowing. They'd finally shooed the children out into the yard just to have room to turn around.

"What do you think, Eli?" Andy Chupp set the cardboard box he was carrying—clearly marked *kich* on the table. "Are the cabinets sound?"

"Some are. Some aren't. There's water damage on the one under the sink, there. And that one—" He pointed to an upper cabinet just to his right. "That one needs fixing to the wall better. You put anything heavy in it, it's going to come down."

Eli had expected the usual frowns and sighs that came when somebody found out repairs were needed.

But Andy only smiled. "*Gut* thing I've got an expert's help, then. I appreciate it. Whatever materials are needed, I'll pay for up front. If you know about how much it'll be, I can go ahead and give you the money today. Or we can square up later, whichever you'd rather."

"Later's fine."

"Later's fine for what?" Hannah walked into the kitchen carrying another smaller box. She was a pretty woman, her dress rounded out gently with her pregnancy. Eli wasn't sure if this would be the Chupps' first baby or if any of the *kinder* swarming the house belonged to them already. He'd given up trying to puzzle out who was who five minutes after his arrival.

"Eli and I are just settling up." Her husband's eyes lit with affection—and concern. "You're not supposed to be carrying things, Hannah. We talked about that."

"No boxes bigger than a loaf of bread, I know. And this one isn't."

"Hannah."

"Well, it's only a little bigger. I'm anxious to get all the kitchen things in here so I can start getting organized." She smiled at her husband, her smile nearly as wide and generous as Trudy's. "You should be happy about that. You'll be wanting to eat, I expect."

"Things may have to stay in boxes awhile yet," Andy told her. "Eli's found some cabinets that need fixing. He's going to see to the repairs for us when he can, but in the meantime it's going to be a little inconvenient."

His wife shrugged good-naturedly. "Just bring in all the boxes, and I'll sort out the things I really need. I'll find a way to make do until our Eli can get around to the job."

Our Eli. The affectionate expression jarred him.

He looked out the window over the sink. Trudy and a flock of small *kinder* were busy in the yard, picking up sticks, raking leaves and pulling weeds from the overgrown flower beds. Leah was helping, and she looked content—happy even—in spite of the crowd. But then, she always was happy when she was with Trudy.

Trudy was standing underneath an oak tree, bright with golden leaves, a rake in one hand. She had on a green work dress today, faded from wear. She'd made a little joke about how raggedy it was when he'd picked her up, but he thought she looked nice in it. The color suited her. As he watched, one of the children said something to her. It must have been something funny because she laughed.

Eli's lips twitched. He knew just what that laugh would sound like—rich and musical. He'd told her back at Ephraim Miller's pond that he liked to see her smile, but that wasn't the half of it. When her face lit up like that, there was something about Trudy Schwartz that caught him right in the belly, like when a quick-riding buggy dipped too fast on a hill.

"Um... Eli?"

He blinked and turned his head to find Hannah regarding him with lifted eyebrows. Andy had disappeared, no doubt gone to haul in more boxes.

"I'm sorry. Did you say something?"

"I was asking if there are any cabinets sound enough for me to use now, or if I'd best wait until you've had time to work on them." Mischief glimmered in her blue eyes. "You were too busy looking at my sister to hear me, I guess."

"Ach..." He glanced back out the window, embarrassed. Trudy was raking leaves now, gathering them up with brisk strong strokes. He looked quickly away. "Leah's out there, too, and sometimes she gets *naerfich* when there are lots of people around. I just—"

Hannah chuckled and held up her hand. "You don't have to explain. I'd be more worried if you weren't watching Trudy."

A fond smile curved Hannah's mouth as she watched her sister toss a handful of leaves at a giggling little boy. "She's so wonderful with little ones. Always has been. Naturally, she's longing to have a family of her own, and it's broken our hearts watching her waiting, with no likely fellow in sight. But we should have trusted *Gott*, shouldn't we? With you and your niece, she'll have a ready-made family right from the start. Such a blessing."

She paused as if waiting for his reply. Instead of answering, Eli shifted his hammer from one hand to the other. He wasn't sure what he was supposed to say, and he desperately didn't want to say the wrong thing.

He wanted Trudy's family to like him.

That realization hit him out of the blue—and startled him so much that he dropped the hammer he was holding. It fell onto his left boot with a resounding thump.

"Oh, dear." Hannah made a sympathetic noise, but her eyes were twinkling. "I'm sorry if I've made you uncomfortable. It's just that you and your sweet niece are answers to this family's prayers, and I wanted you to know."

"Hannah?" Andy called from the living room. "Come show your *daed* and *bruders* where you want the living room furniture!"

"Coming!" Hannah smiled at Eli, and to his astonishment, she reached over and gave his arm a friendly squeeze. "You are very welcome here, Eli Mast," she whispered, giving him a sisterly wink before hurrying into the adjoining room. "Not there, Aaron!" he heard her fussing cheerfully. "I want the sofa in front of the big window!"

A chorus of voices rose, offering advice and arguments, but Eli barely heard them. He was looking back out the window at Trudy. She'd stopped raking and was watching the children play. The *kinder* scampered around the yard, chasing each other in some frenzied game of tag, laughing breathlessly. Leah was among them, running just as fast and laughing just as hard as the rest.

They were stirring up the leaves she'd managed to get into piles, but Trudy didn't seem bothered. She watched the little ones play, a wistful smile on her face.

She glanced toward the window and caught him looking. The sweet smile broadened, and she waved enthusiastically.

Eli's heart lifted. He lifted his own hand in reply, the corners of his mouth quirking upward.

Just then one of the smaller children took a tumble and cried, and Trudy hurried to help him. Eli watched her gather the tiny boy in her arms, comforting him as a *mamm* would do, and for the thousandth time since their day at the auction, that picture of the stair-step *familye* came up in his head.

He wanted that to be real so much that he felt dizzy with it.

Quickly, Eli turned his back to the window. As he leaned over to pick up his hammer, his stomach churned so hard that he almost felt sick. He straightened slowly, kept his eyes on his boots and breathed carefully, in and out.

He knew this feeling. He'd had it often back when he was an apprentice, but it came back sometimes even now when he was working on a particularly difficult piece. It was the desperation of a craftsman who could see beauty he wanted to create—but feared he didn't have the skills to pull it off.

Because for there to be any chance of that family he could see in his head, he needed to talk to Trudy—really talk to her. What she'd said that day in the buggy—about him being the most honest man she knew—that had been keeping him awake at night. Because he hadn't been honest with her at all. Well, not completely.

He'd told Trudy about Abby, but he still hadn't told her everything. He needed to tell her why he'd come to Susie

Raber's looking for a courtship in the first place—and why she'd turned him down flat. He needed to explain about his *aent* and *onkel*, and the pestering bishops, before she found out from somebody else. He needed her to understand how *Gott* had put him together—how he'd never felt suited to marriage. How he still didn't feel like he'd be too *gut* at it.

The difference was, now he wanted to be.

He needed to explain all that. He, Eli Mast, who couldn't seem to string three words together without getting two of them wrong. But he was going to have to do it—and he was going to have to do it soon.

Then he'd see whether Trudy and her family still thought he was the answer to their prayers.

Chapter Ten

A week later, Trudy and Susie were busy in her kitchen, Susie experimenting with yet another cookie recipe and Trudy packing a large basket with a variety of homemade goodies. This Saturday was the bidding picnic to raise funds to settle the last of Caleb King's medical bills so that no debt would be left for his grieving family to deal with.

"I still can't get over the bishop allowing this," Trudy said as she tucked ham sandwiches inside. She'd layered water bottles, cookies, chips and pickles underneath, planning to put the sandwiches on top so they wouldn't get crushed.

"*Ja*, some of the older folks don't like it." Susie quickly transferred hot cookies from the baking sheet to a rack to cool. "Even though Charley's limiting it to our own church members and put out a list of what foods can be included, so the girls won't be tempted to show off. The idea of selling baskets of food for a picnic may be common enough among Mennonites but it's not something we've done here before. I think it's a real *schmaert* idea, though. Besides, we needed to do something. Those last bills came as a surprise to Caleb's family." She set her spatula down on the counter with a sigh. "And since Owl Hollow was already planning their auction for the Stoll child's expenses, it didn't seem wise to have a second one here so soon. The bids for the lunches will raise the amount we need, and it should be fun for the community, too."

"I hope so." Trudy frowned as she rearranged the items more appealingly in the basket.

Susie broke a piece off one of the cookies and tasted it. "This batch isn't quite right, either," she murmured. "Too much molasses. By the way, have you asked Eli to bid on your basket, Trudy?"

"Nee," Trudy shook her head. "I haven't asked him anything, except if he was planning to go."

Surely, Eli understood that he was supposed to bid on her basket. This bidding picnic was a new idea, but everybody seemed clear on how it was supposed to work. Husbands were planning to bid on their wives' baskets, and bachelors could bid on the baskets of their sweethearts. She knew from snippets overheard at church last Sunday that folks were looking forward to this auction for that very reason. There had been much good-natured speculation going on in the kitchen after the noon meal about who was expected to bid on whose basket.

"You'd better ask him," Susie advised now. "Tell him which basket is yours and that, being as how you two are courting, would he please bid on it so you two can eat your lunch together."

"Oh, I don't know..." The idea of asking Eli such a thing made her uncomfortable, especially after this past week. Eli had been acting strange—and she didn't know why.

It had started on the buggy ride back from her sister's new house. Before that, things had seemed all right. He'd agreed to go to the frolic—to please her, he'd said. The fact that he'd cared about pleasing her had pleased her most of all.

The frolic itself had gone well enough. Of course, with all the work to do and all the family buzzing around, there hadn't been much opportunity for the two of them to talk, not without half a dozen people overhearing. But she'd caught Eli watching her a time or two, and the expression on his face had made her heart sing.

Then, right before it was time to leave, when she'd been stacking jars of homemade applesauce in the pantry, Hannah had leaned over and whispered. "I had a little talk with Eli in the kitchen. That man likes you, Trudy. He likes you plenty."

Trudy had been so happy that she'd begged a jar of the applesauce from her sister to take home. She'd planned to save it for a special occasion. Maybe, she'd thought with a happy blush, for the first breakfast she fixed as a married woman.

But on the buggy ride home, he'd been so quiet—even quieter than usual. He hadn't lingered in the afternoons when he'd come by to pick up Leah, either. And he'd never mentioned this picnic until she'd brought it up herself, even though everybody in the community was talking about it.

It seemed impossible to figure out how Eli felt about her—or didn't feel. One minute he was saying something surprisingly sweet, the next he was barely talking to her at all. She still didn't know if she should be planning a wedding or preparing for a future as a Good Apple Girl.

She looked up and found Susie watching her, a compassionate gleam in the older woman's eye.

"If you want Eli to bid on your basket, Trudy, you'd better ask him to. Otherwise you're likely to end up with hurt feelings."

Trudy gave her an exasperated look. "You know, Susie, I've done plenty of asking already. I was the one who brought up the Owl Hollow auction. I've asked him for buggy rides and for walks, and to go to my family's work frolic. If I have to do all the asking, it sure doesn't seem like there's much hope of this courtship going anywhere. What are you going to tell me to do next? Ask the man to marry me?"

She'd meant it as a joke. But to her surprise, Susie didn't laugh.

"It wouldn't be the first time I told a woman to propose."

"Susie!"

The matchmaker chuckled. "Almost any courtship can end in a marriage if you're not too picky about how you get there. Whether it'll be a happy marriage or not—that's a very different question. And a much more important one. Oh, get that horrified look off your face. I'm not suggesting you ask Eli to marry you. In fact," she went on thoughtfully, "I'd say that's the one question I wouldn't ask him, if I were you. Let Eli be the one to open that particular door, Trudy, when he's good and ready."

"If he ever is."

"He might be closer than you think. A little nudging..."

"I'm not asking him to bid on my basket, Susie."

"Fine. If you're determined to be stubborn about it, I'll just do the asking for you. *Nee*," she said when Trudy started to speak. "I'm not matchmaking. Eli and I haven't come to that kind of understanding. Not yet. But I guess a good cook can't help but add a pinch of salt when she sees a dish that needs it. Now quit fussing with that lunch, and let's get our bonnets and shawls. It's past time to go."

"Susie?" Trudy took their bonnets off their pegs and handed Susie hers. "Can I ask you something?"

"Of course."

"The woman you told to propose to the fellow. Is it somebody I know?"

"For shame, Trudy Schwartz," Susie said sternly. "You know as well as I do that gossip is a sin. What would the bishop think? Especially," she added with a twinkle in her eye, "since it was his own daughter I told to do it. Now let's hurry and hitch up the buggy. We're going to be late."

Eli walked away from the neat line of buggies, toward the crowd growing around the Yoder family's largest barn. Leah trotted beside him, looking around at all the people who'd turned out for the picnic auction.

There were a lot of them. The Miller farm wasn't half as crowded as the auction sale had been over in Owl Hollow last week, but it was still far too crowded for Eli's liking. People were everywhere. Most he knew, some he didn't. Yet. But if this pace of socializing kept up, no doubt he'd know every Plain person in the whole community in a week or two.

He wasn't sure how he felt about that. Two auctions, plus the Schwartz family work frolic all in one month seemed like a lot to him. Back in Carroway, he wouldn't have gone to three such events of any sort in a year, much less back-to-back. It had been a smaller community with fewer goings-on, and he'd quietly ignored most of the events they had held.

He'd been more comfortable alone in his workshop—or at home with Leah. But Trudy liked these things, and he liked Trudy. So, here he was.

Where was she, anyway? He'd not seen her yet, and Susie Raber's buggy hadn't been among those he'd passed walking up to the barn. He knew because he'd looked. But likely she'd be along soon, happy as always, smiling at everybody.

Smiling at him.

But only because he still hadn't been honest with her. He'd been cutting short their afternoon visits all week, trying to figure out the best way to explain. After Leah went to bed at night, he'd sat up scribbling sentences on paper, trying to get the words right. He'd practiced explaining out loud, driving away from Susie's in the mornings, when he was alone in the buggy. So far, nothing he'd come up with had sounded anything but *schtupid*.

I don't think I'd be much gut at marriage, but the bishops are pushing me into it, so I don't have much choice. I never thought this courtship would go anywhere, but if I have to get married, I think I'd like to be married to you. The trouble is, I'm pretty sure you wouldn't much like being married to me. Except for Leah, I can't seem to make people happy, no matter how hard I try.

That was honest enough, but if Trudy had any sense at all—and he knew she did—she'd end things then and there. He really didn't want that to happen, so he kept putting it off.

"Leah!" A little girl about the same age ran up to them. One of Trudy's nieces, Eli realized. He recognized her from the children who'd been swarming around Trudy that day, but he couldn't think of her name.

Thankfully, Leah had no such problem. "*Hallo*, Becky!" she said, smiling around the finger she had stuck in her mouth.

"Do you want to come sit with us? My *mamm* said you could if your *onkel* says it's all right. She filled a big basket full of all our favorite things, and my *daed* is going to bid on it. There's enough for you to share, and she even put some of those brownies you liked so much in—the ones with the marshmallows!" The little girl got her invitation out in one breath and waited hopefully.

Leah took her worry finger out of her mouth. "Can I?" she asked Eli.

He looked up to see one of Trudy's sisters—Emma, he thought was her name—smiling and walking in his direction. He lifted a hand politely.

"Sure, if you want to."

Becky bounced up and down. "Do, Leah! We can sit together and help look after my baby brother. It'll be fun!"

Leah's eyes lit up. She loved babies. "Okay!" Hand in hand, the girls raced off together, brushing past Emma.

"Don't fall down and dirty your dresses," she called after them. Then she turned back to Eli. "You don't mind, do you? Us stealing Leah away? All the *kossins* want to sit together, and I packed plenty of food in the basket."

"*Nee*, I don't mind," Eli said. "I appreciate you inviting her."

"*Ja*, I figured you might." To his surprise, Emma winked. "I'm sure Trudy put enough in her basket for Leah, too, but I thought you two might enjoy eating lunch together alone. Or as alone as you can be with everyone around. We're over there under that big oak tree when you're ready to collect Leah. Have fun—and tell Trudy she owes me a favor." With another wink, Emma hurried after the girls.

Eli barely noticed. He was busy playing catch up.

He was supposed to buy Trudy's basket? He hadn't realized that—to be honest, he hadn't thought about how this bidding picnic worked at all. Trudy had wanted him to come, so he'd come. And he'd looked forward to seeing her, assuring himself that it was all right to enjoy another happy day in her company before having the conversation he was dreading.

But, apparently, he was expected to bid on the basket she brought. He mentally did a count of the money in his wallet. Enough, he thought, with relief. Surely, what he had with him would be more than enough. Then again, this was a fundraising auction, so he wasn't entirely sure how much he was expected to pay.

He also had no idea—absolutely none—how he'd know which basket was Trudy's. Forgetting his distaste for crowds, he shouldered through the press of people to where long tables were set up, covered with an assortment of picnic baskets. The auctioneer was already behind the little podium, conferring with Charley Coblentz, the bishop.

The baskets all looked different, but he couldn't tell which one was Trudy's.

Just then he caught sight of Susie Raber in the crowd, but she was talking to some woman he didn't recognize. Trudy wasn't with her.

The auctioneer picked up a basket and stepped toward the podium—and panic tightened Eli's chest.

He had no time to lose.

Quickly, he strode toward Susie, just as the other woman turned away.

"Eli!" Susie regarded him with some mild surprise. "I've been looking for you. We were a little late. We had some trouble with one of the harness straps. Now, listen. There's something I need to tell—"

"Which one?" he ground out desperately.

"What?"

"Which of those baskets am I supposed to bid on? Tell me quick before they get started."

Susie stared at him for a split second, then—to his embarrassment—she sputtered into laughter.

"Well," she said finally. "If this doesn't beat all."

"Folks, let's quiet down now!" The auctioneer was calling from his little platform. "It's near lunchtime, and everybody's good and hungry. Time to start this auction!"

"Did somebody tell you? Or did you figure it out for yourself?" Susie was asking.

He didn't have time for questions. *"Which one?"*

Susie lifted an eyebrow, but amusement twinkled in her eyes.

"It's an oval basket with a lid." She craned her neck. "It's...the third one up, I think. The blue napkin is sticking out a little at the corner. See?"

Relief coursed over him. "*Ja. Ja*, I see it. *Denki*, Susie."

"*Du bisht welcome.*" She eyed him thoughtfully. "Eli, I've been thinking. Maybe I—"

"There you are!" Trudy came up beside them, breathless and beaming. "My, what a crowd! Isn't it wonderful? They should make a lot of money today, and I'm so glad." She shook her head sadly. "The King family has had such a sad time. I'm thankful they likely won't have to worry about those medical bills after today. Where's Leah?"

The auctioneer had started his patter—but the basket up for grabs wasn't Trudy's, so Eli couldn't have cared less. Still, the noise was high, so he leaned closer to her ear to tell her how Leah had gone off with her sister and niece.

But, as he bent his head close to hers, he caught a whiff of a sweet-smelling soap and the lemony starch of her *kapp*, and every thought he had flew out of his head like dandelion fluff on a windy day.

"Eli?" Trudy prompted after a second or two.

He blinked and explained where Leah had gone. He glanced back up front and realized he'd come back to himself just in time. The auctioneer was holding Trudy's basket.

"This one's heavy!" he said. "Says on the tag it's a lunch for three folks. What am I bid?"

"Ten dollars!" a male voice called from across the yard, and Eli turned his head sharply in that direction. He couldn't see who the bidder was. Trudy gave him no clue. She was watching the auctioneer, her cheeks pink and her lips set in a tight line. She looked almost as uncomfortable as he felt.

"Any more bids? No? Ten dollars is a bargain for a lunch

that'll feed three people! Will anybody give me fifteen? All right, then! Going, going—"

"One hundred dollars!" Eli shouted desperately. That wasn't quite all he had in his pocket, but it was most of it.

Silence fell for a few seconds. Then the auctioneer chuckled. "Somebody really wants this one!" A ripple of laughter rolled over the crowd. "Sold!" He handed Trudy's basket off to a woman standing to his left and picked up the next one.

Eli breathed a sigh of relief. That was over with, and Trudy's basket was rightfully his. He looked at Trudy and was taken aback by the look on her face.

She looked astonished, and her cheeks had paled, as if someone had frightened the wits out of her.

His heart sank. What had he done wrong this time? "What?"

"Eli." She seemed to be having some trouble getting words to come out. "You just spent one hundred dollars. On a lunch."

"Ja." That seemed pretty self-explanatory, so he wasn't sure what her point was. "I could've bid more," he admitted. "But I figured that would probably do it." And it had, sparing him from going back and forth with whoever had called out the first bid.

He wondered if Trudy knew who that fellow was.

"But...a hundred dollars? For a lunch?"

He shrugged uneasily. He still didn't understand the problem. *"Ja,* so I guess I'd better go get it, ain't so?"

She blinked. *"Ja,* I... I guess you'd better."

He walked over to the table and counted out one hundred dollars cash into the woman's hand. She tucked it inside a little metal box and handed him the basket with a smile.

"You really did want this lunch," she said. "Trudy Schwartz packed it, didn't she?"

"I sure hope so," he answered sincerely. "No other woman's lunch is worth that kind of money to me."

The woman laughed, glancing over his shoulder. He looked, too, and found Trudy was standing there. Her face was a pretty pink again, and she appeared both pleased and embarrassed.

The woman smiled at them. "Since your basket was one of the first ones sold, you'll have your choice of picnic spots. There's some nice places over by the smaller barn." She shook a teasing finger at them. "But stay well in sight or you might have the bishop coming looking for you."

"All right," Eli nodded shortly. *"Denki."*

"You're very welcome," the woman replied, but she wasn't looking at him. She was looking at Trudy, and her eyes were twinkling.

He led the way out of the tightly packed crowd, breathed a deep sigh of relief and turned to Trudy. "Where do you want to sit?"

She pointed wordlessly to a bench positioned against the smaller red barn, so he walked that way. He set the basket on the ground within handy reach and waited for her to settle herself on the bench before taking his own place.

They were facing the auction, and to his surprise, he saw several people watching them instead of the auctioneer. "What are those folks looking at us for?"

"Because you just paid a hundred dollars for a lunch. For *my* lunch."

Eli felt a tickle of alarm—mingled with exasperation. "Isn't that what we're supposed to do? Bid money for the lunches to raise money?"

"Well, *ja*. But…a hundred dollars is a lot of money. You could have won it for a lot less."

"Maybe. Or maybe that other fellow would have kept on

bidding and running up the price. I didn't like the idea of that, so I bid the top amount I figured I could pay to stop him short." And he had, he thought with some satisfaction.

Her face fell. "Oh, Eli. He'd never have bid up so high. That was my brother, Isaiah. You didn't meet him the other day because he had to work."

Her brother. That was different. "I'm sorry. Did you want him to win it?"

"Nee." Trudy laughed—but it was a strange thick laugh, as if she were trying not to cry. *"Nee,* I didn't want him to win it, and he didn't want to win it, either. He's got a special friend named Sarah, and I'm sure he's hoping to get her basket."

This was why he didn't like things like this, Eli thought irritably. Nothing was ever as simple as it sounded. "Why'd he bid on yours, then?"

"To be kind to me. So I wouldn't feel ashamed. I guess he wasn't sure anybody else would bid on it. Nobody would've...before you."

Eli thought that over. He liked this Isaiah, he decided. He'd never met him, but he already liked him. "Well, I guess it worked out all right, then. Everybody's happy. Or will be," he amended with a grin, "depending on what you've packed in that basket. Let's give thanks, and then we'll eat. Okay?"

She nodded and bowed her head to offer her silent thanks for the food. Eli started to bow his, too, but hesitated for a second longer, watching Trudy.

Her brow was furrowed slightly as she prayed, her hands folded in her lap, the October sun, picking through the golden leaves above them to bring out the lighter notes in her smooth, brown hair.

She looked sweet, he thought. And he liked sitting here with her, just her, away from the crowd. He loved Leah, and never before did he recall being glad when his niece wasn't by his side. But just at the moment, knowing that she was safe and happy with Trudy's sister, he had to admit it was nice to have Trudy all to himself.

He suddenly realized he was staring instead of praying, so he quickly bowed his head.

When he lifted it again, Trudy was waiting. When she saw he was done giving thanks, she leaned over and began to unpack the basket.

The auctioneer had been right. It was a real good lunch, and he couldn't help but notice that Trudy had included things she knew he liked especially—like the cookies he'd remarked on this past week.

She handed him a napkin to spread over his lap and then divided up the food between them. He unwrapped his sandwich and started to take a bite—then stopped. Trudy had made no move to pick up her own sandwich. Instead she was watching him, a serious expression on her face.

Had he missed something? "What are you waiting on?" he asked uneasily. "We've prayed already."

"I feel like I should thank you, Eli. That was…that was a very nice thing you did, bidding so much money on my basket."

Eli nodded cautiously. At least she didn't seem upset, so that was good. "I don't think you owe me any thanks. It's not like you're keeping the money," he pointed out with a smile. "And I get a real *gut* lunch out of the bargain."

Real sweet company, too, he thought, but he didn't dare say that out loud. It sounded good in his head, but no doubt he'd make a hash of it if he tried to say it.

Trudy nodded, but her mouth trembled a little. "I know that, of course. And I guess it's silly of me to care about such a thing, and probably prideful, too. But I just…" Her cheeks flamed pinker. "No fellow would ever have done such a thing, not just to have lunch with me. Not before today."

The men in Hickory Springs didn't have very good sense, Eli thought—not for the first time.

He shrugged. "Nobody ever really wanted to have lunch with me before either," he admitted honestly. "Or if they did, they changed their minds pretty quick once they got to know me." He shifted uneasily on the bench, thinking guiltily of the unpleasant conversation still hanging over their heads. "You might, too."

"*Nee*, never," she assured him, her face bright with earnest sincerity. "I'd never feel so about you, Eli."

"Never's a long day," he muttered. He started to lift his sandwich to his mouth, then sighed and set it back on his napkin.

"Trudy," he said. "I need to tell you something."

Chapter Eleven

Trudy studied Eli with alarm. She didn't like the grim set of his jaw or the way he was forcing himself to look her in the face, although she could tell he wanted to look away.

Then again—her natural optimism bobbed up—whatever he needed to tell her, how bad could it be? The man had just paid a hundred dollars for the lunch she'd made, something she'd certainly never expected. Everybody in Hickory Springs now knew—or soon would—that Eli Mast had his eye on Trudy Schwartz.

That was a heady feeling. If she was honest, there was a bit of *hochmut*, pride, mixed into it—over for once being the woman who was singled out by a man, and in such a showy way. She'd be praying over that this evening, asking *Gott* to forgive her for enjoying it so much.

But pride wasn't all she felt. She also felt joy and hope, and—her gaze rested fondly on Eli's face—a shy affection that was strengthening with every heartbeat.

And going by today's events, Eli must feel something for her, too. Whatever he was stewing over, surely it couldn't be so terrible.

"What's troubling you?" she asked gently.

"I don't… I've never…" He took a breath and started again. "I'd better start at the beginning. I haven't been…

completely honest with you. The truth is, I've never actually planned on getting married." He waited through a couple of heartbeats. "Trudy? Did you hear what I said?"

Trudy nodded woodenly. She'd heard the words, but somehow their meaning didn't quite register. Just at this moment, when the sun was so bright and the world seemed such a beautiful, loving and friendly place, the kind of heart-sickening disappointment these words meant...

Well, it just didn't seem possible.

He was waiting for her reaction. He looked worried, probably expecting her to cry or get angry. Small wonder, since either one of those would have been a very appropriate response to a man who'd led her on like Eli Mast had done.

But she didn't feel...anything. Not yet, although she understood the agony that was likely coming. It was like that stunned moment just after you stubbed a toe, before the pain started.

"Trudy?" His voice sounded ragged.

She tried to gather her wits. "To me, you mean. You don't want to get married *to me*." She didn't make it a question, because she assumed it wasn't one. No man had ever wanted to marry her, so it wasn't like this was anything new.

"*Nee*, it's not you, Trudy." He spoke so fervently that she almost believed him. "I just... I never felt like *Gott* fitted me well for marriage."

But that didn't make any sense. "Then why did you go to Susie's? That first day we met? If you didn't want to get married, why on earth were you looking for a matchmaker?"

"Because of Leah. That's what I need to tell you. I never would have gone to talk to Susie if it hadn't been for Leah."

She listened silently as he talked about how the bishop at his old community hadn't thought he'd be as good a parent to Leah as a married couple. "I know he might be right about that," he admitted roughly. "I know how I am. I'm not so *gut* with most people, and the harder I try, the worse I am. But I am *gut* with Leah, I think."

"*Ja*, you are very *gut* with her," Trudy agreed. The pain was starting now, a slow throbbing in her heart.

"Someone like you would be better, probably," he said. "But I know the couple that want her—they are the *aent* and *onkel* who took me and Abby in. I know how they'd be. They'd mean well, but they wouldn't try to understand her little fears and such, any more than they'd understood me and Abby. I didn't know anything about raising a little girl, but I did my best. But then after our *aent* and *onkel* stirred up some trouble, the bishop said if I wanted to keep Leah with me, I'd need to take a wife."

Trudy nodded slowly. "So you went to see Susie."

"*Nee*, not at first. I left Carroway and settled here because I'd heard Charley Coblentz was an easier bishop to deal with. I only went to see Susie when Charley sided with Jakob Hochstetler, the Carroway bishop. But she wouldn't help me. Because I was honest with her about why I was there and how I felt."

The pain in Trudy's heart throbbed again. So that's why Susie had turned Eli away. Because Eli didn't really want to get married. And she couldn't imagine why he'd be admitting all this to her now, unless he still felt the same way.

Susie had tried to warn her. *You should ask more questions, Trudy.*

Fine, then. She'd ask her questions. Plenty of them, starting now. What did she have to lose?

"Why?"

"What?" He looked confused.

"Why didn't you want to get married? Most Plain people do, don't they? Men and women alike. Then you'd have a partner to help you bring up Leah, and she'd have a *mamm*. Those are good things, ain't so? Besides, you're a member of the church, and you know as well as I do that when a bishop tells you to do something…well—" Trudy made a helpless gesture "—you're supposed to do it, not try to find a way around it. That first bishop, he wasn't telling you to marry anybody in particular, was he? You were free to choose the woman yourself?"

"*Ja*, I was free to choose."

"Then why were you so set against it?" She held her breath as she waited for his answer. Everything depended on what Eli said next.

He shook his head. "I told you. I don't feel like *Gott* suited me for it. It wonders me that I have to explain it to you. You've spent enough time with me yourself to know that already, I'd think."

"You'd think wrong, then."

"It's just that… I'm not… I've never been the kind of man who'd make a good husband. I say all the wrong things. I do all the wrong things. It's not that I mean to. I just don't think the way other people do. Any woman married to me would be signing on for a lot of heartache. I've always done better alone."

"But you're not alone anymore, are you? You have Leah now, and as far as I can see, you make her plenty happy."

"Tell that to Charley Coblentz." Eli scrubbed a hand across his face. "I'm really sorry, Trudy."

The throb in Trudy's heart ached a little deeper. She fixed her gaze on the half-emptied basket at her feet. How had they gone from that amazing auction bid to *I'm really sorry*?

All her life people had told her that pride went before a fall. Today had certainly proved it.

"You're forgiven, Eli." She sighed. "Although I admit,

it's not too pleasant to find out that the only man who ever showed any interest in me is sorry he did."

"Don't say that!"

Eli spoke so sharply that Trudy raised her head and looked at him. He looked back, his hazel-brown eyes narrowed and fierce.

"I never said I was sorry to be courting you, Trudy. I meant *you* should be sorry for courting *me*, and you should be. I've sure made a hash out of it so far."

"I wouldn't say that." Trudy's heart was aching, but the hangdog look on Eli's face made her gentle in spite of her own pain. "*Ja*, you've made a bumble or two. But you were doing pretty *gut* today—at least up until now. When a fellow pays a hundred dollars for a girl's lunch, it makes her feel plenty special."

"That was an accident."

"What? You mean you didn't mean to bid a hundred dollars?"

"*Nee*. I was willing enough to do that. I heard what Caleb King's family went through. They're welcome to what money I have to spare. But I didn't bid it all at once hoping to make you feel special. The back-and-forth was making me uneasy. I just wanted to cut it short and make sure I ended up with your basket in the end."

"Oh." She thought that over. "Would you really have cared so much, Eli? If you hadn't won my basket?"

"*Nee*, not so much." Just as Trudy's heart sank, Eli went on. "Although, I'll say that before I knew it was your brother bidding, I cared a good bit."

He sounded bemused, and in spite of everything, Trudy couldn't help smiling.

"So," she said after a moment or two. "What are we going to do about this?"

"I guess that's up to you, Trudy."

"I see." Trudy looked over the scene in front of her. The auction had just about concluded, and people were scattered around, enjoying their picnic lunches. Going by the satisfied smiles of the auctioneer and the others standing by the now-empty tables, the event had been a great success. "Once word gets out that you and I aren't courting, you may have some trouble with Bishop Coblentz. He can be real stubborn, and even if he wanted to forget about this, it sounds like that other bishop and your *aent* and *onkel* wouldn't let him."

Eli heaved a heavy sigh and nodded. "*Ja*. That's true enough."

Trudy studied him for a second. She wondered if... But surely she couldn't... She shouldn't. And Eli seemed to be done talking.

She should just pick up her basket, walk away and let this whole thing end. Hadn't she been embarrassed enough?

Then again...she knew what Susie would say. *Ask*.

"Can I ask you something, Eli? And you'll tell me the honest truth?"

"You can ask me anything, and I'll answer you best I'm able to."

"If you *were* going to get married—and if you weren't so worried about whether or not you were cut out for it—" Trudy gathered the tattered scraps of her courage "—would I be the kind of woman you'd consider? Remember, you're telling me the truth, no matter what it is."

Eli didn't answer right away, his expression frustratingly unreadable. He looked at her for a long minute in silence. Just when she thought her nerves couldn't stand the suspense another second, he cleared his throat.

"*Ja*, Trudy," he said. "The truth is, I can't think of any

other woman I *would* consider, except you. You're so kind to Leah, and I...well, I like you real well myself."

He liked her real well. He'd said that once before. And Hannah had said the same thing after the work frolic, hadn't she—that Eli liked Trudy plenty—so likely it was true. That was something.

And something, Trudy decided suddenly, was a whole lot better than nothing.

"Well, if that's so—"

"It's so, Trudy."

"All right. Then why don't we?"

"Why don't we what?"

Pretending to be casual, as if her whole life wasn't balancing on the edge of this conversation, Trudy shrugged.

"Why don't we just go ahead and get married?"

It took him a minute. More than a minute, actually, to wrap his mind around the direction this conversation had taken. He'd expected Trudy to fuss. Maybe cry, as women sometimes did when they got really mad or upset. He hadn't looked forward to either of those reactions, but he'd been prepared for them.

He hadn't been prepared for a marriage proposal, and he had no idea what to say. Meanwhile, Trudy sat beside him as calmly as if they were talking about the weather.

"I thought... I guess I didn't do such a *gut* job of explaining this," he said.

"Nee," Trudy responded, adjusting the napkin in her lap. "You explained it fine. You don't want to get married because you don't think you'd suit any woman too well once she got to know you, but you've been backed into a corner if you want to keep Leah with you and away from your *aent* and *onkel*."

He nodded slowly. "*Ja*, that's about it."

"Well, I do want to get married. I always have, but nobody ever wanted to marry *me*. So, maybe you're not the best catch in Hickory Springs, Eli, but I'm not in any position to be picky. You need a wife, and Leah needs a *mamm*. And you just said you liked me fine. Unless…" For the first time, a shadow of doubt crossed Trudy's face. "Unless you were only being nice."

"I wasn't—" He was suddenly aware of movement around them. People were finishing up their lunches and walking about. He didn't want anybody to overhear this conversation. He stood up, dropped his own uneaten sandwich in the basket and reached for Trudy's. "Give me that."

She surrendered her lunch, and he wrapped it clumsily in her napkin and dropped it into the basket on top of his.

"That's a very expensive lunch you're throwing around," Trudy pointed out wryly.

"Come on." Picking up the basket, he motioned her into the little barn and shut the door behind them.

"Eli—" she protested, but he cut her off.

"There are a lot of people out there. I can't think straight when there are too many people, and I have to say this right. Or," he amended realistically, "as close as I can get to right. Because it's important."

Trudy looked at him. After a second, she nodded. "Go ahead. But whatever you need to say, say it as quick as you can."

He didn't blame her for not wanting to linger. The barn was dim after the bright autumn sunshine outside, and it smelled bad. There must have been a pig penned in here at some point. But at least it was quiet, and there were only the two of them here.

"I wasn't being nice, Trudy," he said. "I was being honest. I do like you. That's why I told you all this, even though I knew...that it would hurt your feelings. You have a right to know the truth. And the truth is, you deserve a lot better than a man like me."

"Eli—" Trudy started, but he stopped her again.

"I know you're going to say that no man's ever paid attention to you, but that's not your fault. Sometimes people don't appreciate what's right in front of them." He struggled to find a way to say what he meant. "It's like when I moved here. Back behind Vernon's house, there's a real pretty stand of oak and hickory trees that need thinning. Good wood there, but when I pointed it out to him, Vernon said he'd not even thought about that patch of trees. He saw them every day, Trudy. Every day. But he couldn't see the value of them. That's how it is with you, too, I think. These men in Hickory Springs, they just haven't really seen you yet. But one day, the right fellow—a smart fellow—might come along, one who'll see you for who you are."

"It seems to me that fellow's already come along, Eli. And if it's all the same to you, I think I've waited long enough for a husband." She put her hands on her hips. "So, I guess it's up to you, but you'd better decide pretty quick. It's not going to take too long before somebody notices that we've disappeared, and you know what they'll be thinking."

A sunbeam had found a chink in the wall and was playing over her cheek as she spoke. It was distracting.

"What will they think?"

Trudy gave a little embarrassed laugh. "Oh, what they always think whenever a couple sneaks off together. That you're stealing a kiss or something like that."

A kiss.

His eyes dropped to her lips, and his heart did a funny

flip in his chest. "Would I have to steal a kiss to get one from you, Trudy? Or would you give it to me?"

Even in the dimness of the shed, he could see the pink rising up in her cheeks. She lifted her chin stubbornly. "That depends. Are we getting married or not?"

"What if I said, *ja*, we are?"

"Then I'd kiss you, Eli Mast. If you wanted me to."

He leaned closer—and she didn't move away. Instead, she closed her eyes and tilted her face toward his. And the sweetness of that tugged so hard at his heart that he closed the gap between them and covered Trudy's lips with his own.

The warm softness of the kiss stole both his breath and his wits, and for a few seconds nothing in the world mattered except for Trudy.

Then a blinding light fell over them. Startled, they jumped apart and looked toward the door.

Susie Raber stood framed in the doorway, looking at them with narrowed eyes.

"What's going on in here? As if," she muttered to herself, "I didn't know."

"Eli and I were…talking," Trudy said after an awkward pause.

"I saw what you were doing, and it certain sure wasn't talking." Susie wrinkled her nose. "And in a shed that smells like pig!" She shot Eli an exasperated look. "Come on, Trudy. I've got the buggy hitched up."

Trudy looked back at Eli, clearly uncertain about what to do.

"Go on with Susie. I need to be getting home myself. Lots of things to be done now that we've settled things between us."

Something sparked into her eyes, but when she spoke,

her voice was carefully bland. "*Have* we settled things between us, Eli?"

"I think we have, *ja*."

She smiled at him. "All right, then. I'll see you on Monday."

"Oh, I expect you'll see me before that," he said softly.

Trudy's smile must have been contagious because he was smiling, too. He smiled when he went to find Leah and extracted her with some difficulty from the clutches of Trudy's niece. He smiled the whole buggy ride home.

And he was still smiling much later that night when Leah was asleep in her bed and the small house was quiet, and he was sitting at the kitchen table with paper and a pen, writing a letter to the only address he had for his sister.

Dear Abby, I never thought I'd be saying this, but it looks like I'm going to be getting married...

Chapter Twelve

"Kissing in a pig shed," Susie fussed as she cut the piece of breakfast sausage on her plate into neat little rings. "Of all places! You two could at least have found a better spot."

Trudy froze, a triangle of toast halfway to her mouth. She'd known this conversation was coming. She'd seen it brewing on Susie's face on the ride home from the picnic yesterday, but Susie had held her tongue. She'd waited until today, a visiting Sunday with no church service to prepare for, to bring up the topic.

That delay had given Trudy plenty of time to prepare, and she should've had an explanation ready. But she didn't. The truth was, ever since Eli had kissed her, she hadn't been able to think of much else other than the warm sweet feel of his mouth on hers.

That and the fact that they were now officially engaged.

She'd never actually been kissed before. At her age, most people expected that she'd had a special friend or two in her past, and a kiss or two would have happened naturally.

They hadn't. She'd waited—and hoped—and waited some more, but before yesterday all she'd known about kisses was what she'd read in her books.

Now she knew something else, that some kisses—at least Eli Mast's—were well worth waiting for.

"Well?" Susie prompted. "What do you have to say for yourself?" The matchmaker's lips quirked as she spoke. Trudy didn't think Susie was half so disapproving as she was trying to let on.

"That kiss was...unexpected. Like I told you yesterday, we only went into the shed because Eli wanted to talk to me privately."

"He wanted to talk." Susie snorted. "I've been a matchmaker too long to buy that wagonload of manure, especially after he paid such an amount for your basket. You must have known people were watching the two of you after that. What were they going to think when you two disappeared? You should be thankful I found you before the bishop noticed you were gone. Or your *mamm*!"

Trudy looked down at her breakfast plate meekly, but she was fighting a smile of her own.

She couldn't count the number of times she'd heard her mother fussing at one of her sisters or brothers about slipping away with a sweetheart when they were courting. Now at long last it was her turn.

She didn't mind Susie's scolding one bit.

"So?" Susie walked to the stove and poured herself another cup of coffee. "What was so important that you and Eli needed to *talk* about it in the Miller's pig shed?"

"He wanted to tell me the real reason he came to see you that day. How he didn't want to get married, but the bishops were pushing him into it."

Susie's back stiffened. When she turned around, the humor on her face had shifted into a sharp interest. "He finally told you about that, did he?" She walked back to the table and sat down with a sigh. "Well, that's a relief. I haven't liked keeping that from you, Trudy. I hoped Eli would tell you himself, but he sure took his time about it."

"He said he wanted to be honest with me."

Susie stirred her coffee without taking her eyes off Trudy's face. "I've been meddling in couples' love lives for quite a few years now. In my experience, there are only two reasons a man tells a woman something like that after keeping it to himself for so long. Either he wants to break things off and figures that's the easiest way to do it, or he's had a change of heart and wants to start things off on the right foot going forward."

"We're getting married," Trudy announced—then popped a forkful of Susie's fluffy scrambled eggs in her mouth.

Susie leaned back in her chair. "Is that so?" She sipped her coffee thoughtfully. "So he proposed to you? In a pig shed?"

Trudy opened her mouth to say yes—then stopped. Had Eli proposed? Not…exactly. She'd proposed to him, sitting on the bench outside.

The truth was, Eli *had* been trying to break things off. As that fact registered, a little chill ran up Trudy's spine.

Fortunately, Susie didn't notice. "He sure doesn't seem to have thought it through very well. I've known men to propose in some not-so-romantic spots, but this takes the cake." She studied Trudy over the rim of her coffee cup. "I'd have thought it would bother you. Not exactly the kind of proposal that happens in those books you like."

Nee, it wasn't. And in those books, the girl didn't have to do the proposing, either. Trudy shifted uncomfortably on the hard wooden chair. "Why should it bother me? Weren't you the one telling me that those books aren't realistic?"

Susie nodded slowly. "*Ja*, that's true. It's good to be realistic, and Plain fellows and romantic notions don't generally go together. Our menfolk are practical, and they expect their wives to be the same. The only time most of them are ever romantic is when they're courting. Sounds like our Eli's not even very romantic, then. I mean—" she gave an expressive little shrug "—a pig shed. Really?"

She wished Susie would quit harping on that. Every time she brought it up, Trudy's warm fluttery excitement about Eli's kiss grew a little colder.

She got up and carried her plate to the counter. She'd lost her appetite.

"Eli needs a wife," she said quietly as she cleaned her plate. "Leah needs a *mamm*. Maybe he's not head over heels in love with me, but he told me he...likes me real well. And I like him, too. That's enough for me."

To her surprise, Susie came up and put an arm around Trudy's waist. "Well," she said gently, "you can't get much more realistic than that. But, you know, there are two sides to being realistic. One side is knowing what's too much to expect. But the other side is knowing what you can't live without, what you've every right to expect. There's ditches on both sides of every road, Trudy. Just take care you stay in the middle."

For some reason, Susie's shift from sharp to gentle brought unexpected tears to Trudy's eyes. "You're a strange matchmaker, Susie. First, you won't even help Eli when he asks, and now you sound like you're trying to discourage us from getting married."

Susie chuckled sadly and gave Trudy's waist an affectionate squeeze before moving away. "There's a lot more to matchmaking than just hustling a couple toward a wedding. Now move aside. I'll finish up the breakfast dishes." She nodded toward the kitchen window where a buggy was just pulling into the yard. "Your fellow's here for a Sunday visit. Send Leah inside. She can play with those toys I have in the cupboard while I read through *The Budget*. I expect you and Eli have plenty of things to talk over, and that'll be easier without a little one underfoot."

"*Denki*, Susie." Trudy smiled happily, her eyes lingering on Eli. He'd stopped the buggy and was setting the brake.

"I'm happy to help." The older woman shot Trudy a stern look, but her eyes twinkled. "Contrary to what you might think, I'd like to see you two make a match of it, so long as you'd be the happier for it—both of you. So take your time and talk all you like. But no more ducking into sheds, you hear? Your *mamm* would never let me hear the end of it." She flapped the dish towel at Trudy. "Now, get."

Eli had been sneaking glances at the door as he unhitched his gelding, so he knew the minute Trudy came outside. Even if he hadn't been keeping such a close eye, he thought he'd have known anyway. Funny how the whole world seemed a little brighter once Trudy stepped into it.

Leah, who was waiting impatiently for him to finish up with the horse, had been watching the door, too. She clapped her hands happily.

"There's Trudy!" she crowed. Then she looked up at her *onkel* hopefully.

He smiled. "Go ahead."

Leah sprinted toward Trudy, who hurried down the steps to meet her, smiling that familiar generous smile. She didn't seem the least bit unhappy to have an unexpected visit from the child she took care of every day. And Leah had been looking forward to this ever since he'd announced his plans at breakfast. She'd pestered him all morning, anxious for them to be on their way, which was why he was arriving a little earlier than he'd planned.

He couldn't fault the child for being excited. Not when he was feeling much the same way.

Well, excited and a little *naerfich*. He'd never had to face a woman after kissing her before, and he wasn't entirely sure what he was supposed to say. He wished there was somebody he could ask, but this wasn't the sort of thing folks talked about. At least not with him.

All he could do was try his best—and hope Trudy was in a forgiving mood.

He finished up with the horse and lingered a moment near Susie's hitching post. He had his back to Trudy and Leah, but he could hear them chattering to each other, a pleasant, happy sound. He stared over the field to Miller's pond, sparkling lazily in the morning sunshine and balled his hands into anxious fists.

"Help me, *Gott*," he murmured. He felt a little embarrassed asking God to help him with something as silly as this—something that seemed to come so naturally to other men. But he knew he needed the help, and he had nobody else to turn to. "Help me to get this right."

Then he squared his shoulders, turned and walked across the yard.

To his surprise Trudy was standing alone, waiting for him by Susie's back steps. She had her hands clasped in front of her apron—her dress was plum-colored today, and he liked the way the color touched off the reddish tints in her hair.

He stopped short, halfway across the yard. He'd nearly forgotten one of the main reasons for this visit.

"Eli?" Trudy looked at him questioningly.

How *schtupid* of him, he thought disgustedly. He'd thought out half a dozen ways to do this, and none of them had involved forgetting the whole plan as soon as Trudy came out of the house. After all the work he'd put in, he was wrecking it.

He strode back toward the buggy, rummaging in the back seat for the small parcel he'd stowed there.

Trudy had followed him, her brows drawn together over her nose. "Is something wrong?"

A shaft of bright sunlight was playing over her face. "You have freckles," he blurted out. A spatter of light golden-brown dots covered her nose and cheeks. How had he not noticed that before?

She blinked at him. "I guess so."

"There's no guessing about it. You do." He liked them. They were cute, and the way they were sprinkled across her nose and cheeks reminded him of cinnamon on a piece of buttered toast. Seemed like everything about Trudy reminded him of something sweet. Something good.

"Is that a problem?" For some reason, she looked slightly exasperated. "Me having freckles?"

He frowned, confused. "*Nee*, of course not." Had he already said something wrong?

"Do you want to sit on the front porch?" Trudy suggested after a second. "Susie said she'd watch Leah for us if you wanted to...talk."

"That was nice of her. *Ja*, we've got plenty to talk about, I guess." He followed her around the front of the house, to Susie's small front porch. It held two comfortable rocking chairs.

Eli waited for Trudy to choose the one she wanted first, then he took the other, setting the package in his lap. He wasn't quite sure how or when to give this to her. He'd wait and see if an opportunity presented itself.

They sat in silence for a minute or two. Trudy was rocking her chair, and it squeaked a little.

"Have you told Leah?" she asked.

"About what?"

Trudy's cheeks darkened. "About…you know…us. About our plans."

That was why he'd never noticed the freckles, he realized. Trudy was always blushing, and they were much harder to see when her face went pink like that.

"Oh," he said, realizing she was still waiting for an answer. "*Nee*, I haven't. I wanted to see you first. Make sure you were still… Make sure you hadn't changed your mind."

Trudy took a breath and tightened her hands in her lap. "I haven't changed my mind. Have you?"

The relief of her answer turned his legs to jelly and made him glad he was sitting down. He hadn't realized how tense he'd been, how worried, until now. "I'll not be changing my mind. I don't, usually, once I've made it up, not without a real good reason. People say…" He didn't like telling her this, but he supposed she ought to know up front. "People say I can be *schtubbich*," he admitted uncomfortably.

Trudy didn't seem too worried. "People say the same thing about me."

"I don't think that's bad," he assured her quickly. "Not so long as you've thought everything over careful-like beforehand. When you've figured out what's best to do, it only makes sense to stick to it."

She was watching him and listening closely. She wasn't exactly smiling, but her lips were curved up just a little at the corners as if she didn't dislike what she was hearing.

As if she didn't dislike him.

"That's a very good point. So, since we're both *schtubbich* enough to stick to this plan, I suppose we should tell Leah. I promised her I'd spend some time with her after we talked a bit. Maybe we could tell her then? Together?"

He nodded. "She'll be happy. She nearly bounced out of the buggy coming here because she was going to get to see you." He hesitated. "I was a little worried, though. We didn't have much time to talk after… I wasn't sure how you were feeling about…everything."

I wasn't sure how you were feeling about me. That's what he wanted to say, but as usual he couldn't seem to manage to say exactly what he meant.

He suddenly remembered the package in his lap. "Here." He pushed it into her hands.

She looked down at it. "What is it?"

"A present. Open it."

Slowly, Trudy unwrapped the paper, and as his gift came into view, she caught her breath.

"Oh, Eli. It's beautiful!"

He looked at the small perfectly polished box he'd made for her, and he smiled. "*Ja,*" he said matter-of-factly. "It is."

She turned it over in her hands, admiring the leaves he'd carved carefully on the sides. Not too fancy, but graceful. And he'd hidden pears among them, chiseling their shapes out gently so that their roundness showed.

"But it's more than pretty. It's useful. Here, I'll show you." He lifted the lid, showing her the little hinges that held it firm. "It fits snug, even without a latch, so if you knock it off the table, it won't fly open. And see? I've put a divider in so you can separate things if you like. I didn't know what you might like to keep in there."

She ran a gentle finger along the smooth maple, but didn't speak. He waited a second, then said, "If you don't like it, I can make you something else."

She looked up at him then, and he was surprised to see tears glimmering in her eyes. *"Nee,"* she said thickly. *"Nee,* I love it. This was so kind. *Denki,* Eli."

He considered her dubiously. "If you love it, why are you crying?"

She snuffled a wet laugh. "Women cry sometimes when they're happy."

"Ah." He nodded, relieved. "You're happy, then?"

She looked at him and smiled—a real smile this time, the one he liked best. The one that plumped her cheeks and made her eyes sparkle brighter. "*Ja*. You shouldn't have worried driving over here, Eli. I'm happy with what we've decided. Truly."

The words were simple. Plain and easy to understand. There was nothing the least bit fancy about them. But he could tell she meant them—and somehow that hit him in the chest in a way that was painful and pleasant all at once.

"Let's go on and talk to the bishop, then. Today," he added recklessly. Suddenly, he wanted to be married to Trudy as fast as he could be.

Before she changed her mind.

"We can't. Not today. Charley's out of town until Wednesday," she told him. "He's visiting a sick friend in Pennsylvania."

"Oh."

"I'm sorry. I know you'd like to get this settled as soon as possible so there's no question about Leah."

For once, I wasn't thinking about Leah at all. I was only thinking about you.

Those words rang so loudly in his head that for a minute he thought he'd said them out loud. Which would have been a disaster, more likely than not.

Trudy had understood why he'd come to Susie's looking for a wife, and she'd agreed to marry him. That was enough. If he started talking too much, he'd likely ruin everything.

He didn't want to ruin everything. Not this time.

Not with Trudy.

So he only nodded. "That's right," he said.

Something flickered in her eyes at his words, but she nodded pleasantly enough. "Well, we'll get things started as soon as the bishop is back in town. And I'm willing to get married as soon as it can be arranged."

"You'll need time, though," he said. "To plan the wedding and all."

Trudy shook her head. "Not that much time."

"But—"

"I'm not a very young bride," Trudy pointed out sensibly. "And, like you said, you need this marriage settled quickly, for Leah's sake."

He hadn't said that. She had. But it was true, so he nodded.

"My parents have already dealt with my sisters' weddings and helped with my brothers," Trudy went on. "It shouldn't break their hearts for me to have only a small one. People do that all the time, for second marriages. I think it's more appropriate for an older couple, don't you? A small wedding? Well," she added with a shrug, "as small as it can be. I have a pretty big family."

That sounded wonderful. A simple wedding, small and quick, without so many people—so many strangers—expecting him to talk to them.

Ja, that suited him real well.

But even he knew enough about weddings to know that it wasn't his decision to make. Wedding details got decided by the women.

"Whatever you want is fine with me," he said. "And not just about the wedding. I'm... I've not much to offer, I guess. I've told you that. You're not getting much of a bargain with me. But I do... I really do appreciate you."

"You appreciate me." Trudy repeated the words very softly. She dropped her eyes back to the box he'd made for her, but before she did, he caught that flicker in her eyes again.

He wasn't sure why it had been the wrong thing for him to say, but apparently it had. He felt an all too familiar frustration.

"I do, *ja*," he repeated doggedly. "I want you to know that once we're...once we're married, I'll do my best for you, Trudy. I'll work hard, and I'll see that you never want for anything."

She looked up, but not at him. She gazed over the rolling fields surrounding Susie's house, her generous mouth still and straight. Then she sighed.

"Well, I don't want much, Eli," Trudy said. "Not anymore. So I expect we'll get along just fine." She stood up. "But maybe it would be better for us to wait to tell Leah until after we've talked with Charley. Don't you think?"

He stood up, too. "Whatever you want," he repeated, hoping that was the right thing to say.

Maybe it was because she smiled—a little. But an uneasy feeling started up in Eli's stomach.

He wished the bishop hadn't taken that trip to Pennsylvania.

Chapter Thirteen

The following Thursday morning, Eli studied Vernon, sitting across from him in the workshop of the furniture store.

"Nee," he said. "I'll work the front counter if you want me to, but I'm not doing demonstrations."

"Englischers like that, though. Seeing the craftsman at his work. They'll be more likely to linger in the store and buy things. Besides, what harm could it do?"

"Plenty. You know how jumpy I get around people. I'd likely slice a finger off, and how would your *Englischers* like that? *Nee*, no demonstrations."

Vernon huffed an impatient sigh. "You are a stubborn man, Eli."

"Runs in the family." Eli lifted his coffee cup to hide a smile.

He'd come in this morning to discuss work with his *kossin*, and they were negotiating Eli's role in the business going forward. Eli had suggested the talk. He might not know much about marriage, but he knew that when a man made up his mind to take a wife, he needed to have his finances in order.

And Eli's mind was made up. He prayed Trudy's was, too. So far, she hadn't backed out of their agreement—although he'd held his breath every time he'd seen her.

He'd sent word to Charley Coblentz that he wanted to meet with him as soon as it was convenient. Once that meeting was done, and their engagement was announced in church, he'd feel better. The wedding would follow soon after, as quick as Trudy's family could pull off the arrangements. Three weeks was the usual amount of time. He could wait three weeks.

In the meantime, since their talk last Visiting Sunday, he'd limited the time he spent with her, pleading work or some other obligation whenever he picked Leah up in the afternoons. Not because he'd wanted to. He wanted nothing more than to spend time in Trudy's company. But if they were together very long—especially with him feeling so *naerfich*—he'd surely say something the wrong way or do something *schtupid* and ruin everything without meaning to.

He didn't want to ruin this. It would be easier, he told himself, once they'd been announced at church. Even better once they were safely married. He'd still mess up, he was sure, although he intended to make it his business to learn how to make Trudy happy. But once they were officially a family, he was at least guaranteed the opportunity to make things right.

And he would. He'd promised himself that, as fiercely as he'd promised himself that he'd always look after Leah. With *Gott*'s help, he'd always make things right with Trudy, somehow.

He'd start by providing as well for her as he possibly could. He looked into his near-empty coffee cup.

"No demonstrations. But I think opening the second store in Owl Hollow is a good idea, and I'll make sure you have the inventory for it. And I'll work the counter some, if you need me to."

"I like the sound of that, but when are you going to have

time to make that much more furniture? You're real *gut*, Eli, but you're slow."

"I'm careful."

"Same thing. I want quality work, and yours is the best I've seen. But that takes a lot of time. One man supplying two stores? I don't see it working out."

"I can make it work."

Vernon scratched his beard. "Maybe now you could. But things will soon be changing. Wives and children take up a good bit of time. Trudy's going to want to see you now and again, you know."

Eli's insides went warm and gooey the way they always did when he thought about Trudy being his wife—and of the children they might have. "Maybe she will." He hoped so. He thought it over. "I'll take on an apprentice."

Vernon lifted an eyebrow. "You said you wouldn't do that."

"I will now. Like you said, things are changing. Find one, and I'll get started training him. But no big talkers," he added hastily. "Get a quiet boy who's *schmaert* and knows how to follow directions."

"All right. I heard one of the Yoder boys had apprenticed with old Sam Byer, but Sam's health is failing and he's getting out of the business. Maybe I'll talk to him."

"I'd rather it be somebody who hasn't picked up a plane before. Easier to teach him right the first time."

"But it'd save time if—" Vernon's argument was interrupted by a heavy knock on the door. He peered through the doorway. "We're closed until—" He stopped abruptly. "It's Charley Coblentz. What's the bishop doing here?"

"He's likely here to talk to me," Eli admitted sheepishly.

"Ah!" Vernon's face creased into a smile, and his eyes twinkled. "I guess I'd better answer the door, then!" He winked. "Want me to walk slow so you can sneak out the back?"

"Let the man in, Vernon."

He was surprised Charley had come by so quickly—not that he was complaining. The sooner everything was settled, the better. He just hoped Vernon wouldn't hang around. Conversations with a bishop were uncomfortable enough without his cousin making jokes.

As Charley strode quickly through the showroom toward the workshop, Eli frowned. He didn't look like a bishop who was coming to discuss a wedding. He looked flustered, and he was clutching a letter in his hand.

"Eli," Charley said as soon as he reached the workshop. "We need to talk." Vernon was two steps behind him, but without so much as a blink Charley shut the door in Vernon's face. "Alone," he added firmly. Then turned to face Eli.

"I've had a very troubling letter, Eli."

"From my *aent* and *onkel*, I'm guessing. If you got my message as well, you'll know that they shouldn't be causing trouble much longer."

Charley shook his head. "The letter's not from them. It's from your sister, Eli. It's from Abby." He held out the envelope. "I think you'd better read it."

"How does this look?" Leah poked a crumpled bit of pink material under Trudy's nose.

Trudy glanced over from her own sewing to check the simple running stitches Leah was practicing. "You're doing better and better!"

Leah smiled and settled back in her chair under the window in Susie's living room. Trudy watched her, the dress she'd been working on forgotten in her lap.

Leah was doing real well. Usually she resisted new tasks,

but she'd not balked a bit when Trudy had suggested she try making some stitches. That was progress.

Leah glanced up and saw her watching. "*Denki* for teaching me, Trudy. I like sewing!"

Trudy laughed. "Well, that's *gut*. When you grow up and have a family of your own, there'll be plenty of it to do. My *mamm* was always sewing or mending in the evening, at least until we girls got big enough to help her."

"Did your *mamm* teach you to sew? Like you're teaching me?"

A silly lump rose up in Trudy's throat. *"Ja,"* she managed after a second. "She did."

Leah's thread had slipped out of the eye of the needle, and she frowned as she attempted to rethread it. Trudy watched the struggle without offering to help. For one thing, that was how children learned best—working through a difficulty on their own, if they could. It was a positive change, she thought, that Leah didn't immediately ask for help.

For another, she was glad for the opportunity to deal with the feelings stirred by Leah's innocent question. Teaching a daughter to sew was a *mamm*'s task. Leah was just at the right age for it—four or five was when the lessons usually started. Leah was a bright, careful girl, so Trudy had decided to try her with a real needle and thread right off instead of a plastic needle and yarn. She was doing so well that after teaching her a few other stitches, Trudy would graduate her to making simple, useful things. Like a pot holder, maybe, or a very easy quilt square.

Once Eli and Trudy were married, it would be Trudy's job to teach Leah sewing and dozens of other tasks, just as her *mamm* had taught her. She'd enjoy that—and it was sensible and practical to train children to help as early as possible. As families grew, Plain mothers carried a heavy workload at home, and they needed their daughters' help, just as the men needed the help of their sons. It was pleasant, everyone working together, and it helped children develop a sense of responsibility as well as training them for the roles they'd fill later in life.

The idea—of being a *mamm* to Leah and other *kinder* as well, if *Gott* willed it, of being trusted with the task of guiding and teaching them—that made a happy warmth settle in Trudy's heart.

"Why don't you have a family, Trudy? Like your *mamm*?"

Trudy blinked. Leah had managed to thread the needle and was busy with her stitches again, frowning down at her work as she asked the question.

"Well, because I'm not married," Trudy pointed out. *Yet*, she added silently.

"Do you want to get married?"

Trudy hesitated. Should she point out that this wasn't exactly a question that should be asked? Probably. But given the circumstances…

"*Ja*," she said softly. "I'd like to get married someday. I'd like that very much."

"My *onkel*'s not married," Leah pointed out.

"That's true," Trudy agreed solemnly. "He isn't." She smiled as she picked up the fabric in her lap. Was Leah trying her hand at matchmaking?

"He doesn't want to get married," Leah announced. "Not ever, he says. I asked him. He says he's happy like he is, with just me for his family." She looked up, her little brow crinkled. "My thread's too short. What should I do?"

Trudy swallowed. "You make a knot and start a new thread. Here, I'll show you." Setting her own work aside, she helped Leah tie off the stubby thread and unwound another length of thread from the spool.

Once she had the child started again, she stood up. "I think I'd like a cup of tea. Would you like some lemonade and maybe a sugar cookie?"

"*Ja! Denki*, Trudy."

"You keep practicing your stitches, and I'll get our snacks ready in the kitchen. All right?"

Leah nodded and bent back over her sewing.

In the kitchen, Trudy went about the job of brewing tea, but her thoughts weren't on the everyday task. She kept turning Leah's words over and over in her mind.

He doesn't want to get married. Not ever.

She'd known that already. Eli had told her so himself—that he'd never have considered marriage if it hadn't been for the bishops' interference and the danger of losing Leah.

Her *bruders* hadn't been like that, not at all. The Schwartz boys had enthusiastically chased girls from the time they hit their teens until they'd picked out the sweethearts who would later become their wives. For a while there, it had been hard for Trudy to keep up with who they were driving home from singings. There seemed to be a different girl every few weeks. In fact, it had become a family joke.

Her sisters' special friends had been much the same. They'd hung around the house persistently, turning up whenever there was the slightest excuse for a visit. Trudy was always setting extra plates for supper because some lovesick fellow had shown up and volunteered to help one of the men with some task—all to see whatever Schwartz girl he had his eye on.

That girl had never been Trudy, of course. And now, with Eli—

The familiar sound of a buggy rolling into the yard startled her, drawing her attention to the window. Why would Susie be home from the bakery so early?

To her surprise, it wasn't Susie at all. Eli leaped out of the buggy and strode toward the house.

Trudy switched off the stove and went to the door, throwing a cautious look at Leah as she passed by the living room doorway. The little girl was still absorbed in her stitching, so Trudy eased open the back door and waited for Eli on the steps.

Something had happened. She wasn't sure what, but judging by the stunned look on his face and the fact that he'd left his workshop in the middle of a workday morning, there had to be some kind of trouble brewing.

"What is it?" she asked as soon as he came within earshot. "What's wrong?"

He stopped at the base of the steps, looking up at her. "The bishop came by the shop today."

"Oh!" She knew Eli had left word with Charley's family that he wanted to speak to the bishop as soon as possible once he got back. "Is there a problem with arranging the wedding?"

"*Nee,* we never talked about that. He'd had a letter from my sister. From Abby." He looked down at an envelope he held in his hand. "I still don't know what to think about it. Abby wasn't much on bishops, and she never joined the church. Why would she write to Bishop Coblentz and not to me?"

He spoke quietly, evenly, but Trudy heard the puzzled hurt in the question. She went down the steps and laid a gentle hand on Eli's arm.

"I don't know, Eli. I think she should have. But even so, this letter is *gut* news. Now you know your sister's alive and—" A troubling thought occurred to her. "Oh, Eli! Is the letter about Leah? Does Abby want to take Leah away from you?"

"*Nee.* And she doesn't want anybody else to, either. Here." He held out the letter. "I'm no good at explaining. You'd best read it for yourself."

Trudy's hands trembled as she slid the folded paper out of the envelope. The writer's familiar style of handwriting—the sort taught in most Amish schoolhouses—made a shocking contrast to the words. The letter was direct to the point of being rude—all the more unsettling because it was addressed to Charley Coblentz, a man usually treated with respect.

Abby was outraged that the bishops were threatening to take Leah from her brother's care, and she made it very clear that if they kept on with this plan, she'd come back and take Leah away for good.

And I will raise her Englisch, the letter went on. *I promise you that. So you'd best decide which you think is worse—Leah being raised Plain by my brother or Leah being raised Englisch by me, because those are your only choices.*

Trudy's heartbeat sped up as she skimmed through the letter—and then stopped with a jolt as one underlined sentence jumped out at her.

I don't want my brother forced into a marriage he doesn't want with a woman he doesn't love.

She read the sentence twice. Then she quietly folded the letter and slid it back in the envelope. "I see. What did Charley say?"

"That it's over, Trudy." He looked as though he couldn't quite believe it. "They won't take Leah from me now. Charley says he respects a mother's right to choose who raises her child, but I think it was the threat Abby made to come and take Leah back that tipped the balance." He shook his head. "Abby always did know what button to push. She may not always say things the nicest way, but she never says anything she doesn't mean." He sighed. "I guess we have that much in common."

Trudy nodded, but she was barely listening. She was focused on the words he'd said first, trying to accept the finality of them.

It's over, Trudy.

Ja, it was. It was over—for her. All her hopes and plans and dreams.

Just like that.

Chapter Fourteen

Eli didn't notice—at first—that Trudy had gone quiet. When he finally did, he stopped mid-sentence.

Maybe he'd been talking too much, not letting her get a word in edgewise. He didn't usually chatter so, but today the words were bubbling out. Probably because he felt like an anvil had been lifted off his back.

Abby was alive. He didn't know why she hadn't written to him, and that troubled him, but she was alive and obviously had been receiving his letters. As Trudy had pointed out, that was *gut* news.

But the best news was that now everything was settled. Leah would be staying with him. The relief of that had made his knees wobbly.

Did Trudy think it strange that he'd driven all the way out here in the middle of a workday to share this news with her? It would've made more sense to wait until it was time to pick Leah up. But if he'd stayed at the furniture store he'd have been so distracted by the prospect of talking this over with Trudy that he wouldn't have been able to pay the proper attention to his work anyhow.

That was the first thing he'd thought about, once the reason for Charley's visit came clear. Telling Trudy. He couldn't wait to see her smile, see her eyes light up as he shared his joy with her. As happy as he was, his happiness hadn't felt complete—not until Trudy was included in it.

He waited for her to say something, but she didn't. She only looked at him, her eyes wide, and her face so milky white that her freckles stood out.

He frowned. Reaching out a gentle finger, he touched her cheek. "What's wrong, Trudy?"

Her eyes widened a little more, then she shifted—very slightly—away from his touch.

"Nothing's wrong." Her voice sounded almost normal, but that strange, stricken look stayed on her face. "I'm real glad for you and for Leah, too. This is the very best thing that could have happened. She loves you so, and you're doing such a good job of raising her. How *schmaert* of your sister to think of writing to the bishop."

"Abby's always been *schmaert*. About some things. And always about how to get her own way."

"Now you can have your way, too," Trudy said quietly.

"Well, *ja*. I can keep Leah with me, with no more trouble. I still can't quite believe it."

"That's true, of course. But I meant...now you don't have to get married, after all."

"Ach." So that was what she was thinking. "Well, *nee*, I guess I don't. But—"

"Wait here for a minute," Trudy interrupted. She vanished inside, leaving Eli staring at the closed door.

What was happening? He hadn't come here with the idea of breaking things off with Trudy. That hadn't even entered his mind.

Had he said something wrong? He was desperately going over their conversation in his head when she reappeared—carrying the little box he'd made for her. She held it out with a tight smile.

"This was a very kind gift, Eli, but I don't think I should keep it, now that we aren't getting married. You put so much work into it, that I… Take it." When he didn't budge, she wiggled the box. "Please."

He shook his head, focusing instead on her face, trying to figure out what to say to make her hear him. "I don't… I didn't come here to ask for that back. I just… I wanted to tell you the good news."

Her lips tipped up. He usually loved Trudy's smiles, her big bright, generous smiles, but he didn't love this one. It was small and sad, and it didn't reach her eyes.

"That you're not going to be forced into a marriage?"

Forced into a marriage. The words stirred a memory, and his blood went cold. Abby had written something to the bishop about him not wanting to get married, that he shouldn't be forced into it. Something like that, he couldn't remember exactly what. He'd barely skimmed the letter once he knew the result of it. He'd been too intent on sharing his *gut* news with Trudy to take the time.

And then he'd handed that letter to Trudy and told her to read it. No wonder she was acting this way.

"Trudy, I didn't mean to hurt your feelings." He reached for her, but she moved away—after slipping the box into his outstretched hand. "I'm sorry."

"Don't be. Today's not a day to be sorry, Eli. Today's a day to be thankful. Leah gets to stay with you, and you don't have to get married. Not unless…" She paused, her eyes fixed on his. "Not unless you want to."

Eli looked back at her, forgetting to breathe. Because, *ja*. He wanted to.

He wanted to marry Trudy Schwartz. He'd known that for a while, deep down, and the certainty of it had only strengthened. He wanted that family he kept picturing—or whatever version of it *Gott* saw fit to give them.

He'd not known quite what to do with these feelings that had taken over his heart—he still didn't. He'd loved—really loved—only a few people before. His parents. Abby. And, of course, Leah.

But he'd never loved anyone like he did Trudy, and he had no idea how to make her understand that. He didn't have the words to tell her, to explain, and while he was searching for them, the hope flickered out of Trudy's face.

She took a step backward, inside the door. "You'd better get back to work. If you stay much longer, Leah will see you and she'll wonder why you're here so early. Unless you're ready to explain everything to her, about her mother and that letter and…us, maybe it's best she doesn't know."

Another sad small smile, then Trudy went into the house, closing the door softly behind herself.

Eli stood on the steps for a minute, unsure what to do. He knew what he wanted to do. He wanted to bang on the door—to make Trudy come out and listen to him until she understood how he felt. About her. About them, together.

That was the trouble. Even if he could get Trudy to keep talking to him, what good would it do if he didn't know what to say? How could he explain how he felt when he didn't really understand those feelings himself? And who could understand them? They were a bewildering muddle—strong and tender, while at the same time hopeful and terrifying. He felt more confused and yet more deep-down certain than he ever had in his life.

Because these feelings he had for Trudy—as mixed up as they were—they rang true. At the bottom of it all, he loved her. He didn't blame her for not believing him, but he did.

As he trudged back to his buggy, his heart hurt with every

beat. It had hurt like this the day his parents died. And the night he realized Abby had left home for good. And again, when she'd left Leah with him, and he'd looked at the tiny girl sleeping in a makeshift pallet he'd fixed out of an old quilt and realized this poor *kind* was stuck with him—Eli Mast—and that the best he could do would never come close to being what she deserved.

He hadn't been able to change those things. He hadn't been able to fix them. He didn't know how to fix a bungled courtship, either. But—a flicker of hope stirred in his heart.

Nee, he didn't know how to fix things with Trudy. But he knew someone who might.

Fifteen minutes later, he halted his panting horse in front of Smucker's Bakery and ran inside. Ignoring the squawks from the woman behind the counter, he barreled past the waiting customers into the overheated kitchen.

Susie was working alone, pulling a tray of cookies out of the oven. She glanced over at him, startled, her face flushed pink from the heat.

"Eli! What on earth are you doing here?"

"I want to marry Trudy Schwartz. You're a matchmaker, ain't so? Make the match. You just tell me what to do to show Trudy how much I love her, and I'll do it. Once Trudy understands that, if she doesn't want me..." Even saying that made him flinch, but he pressed on, "Well, if she doesn't, there's nothing either one of us can do about it, I guess. But she's going to know how I feel, and I need you to help me figure out how to tell her. And this time I'm not taking no for an answer."

Susie set the hot cookie sheet down with a clatter and turned, her hands fisted on her hips. She swept him from top to toe with a long hard look.

And then she smiled.

"Well, it took you long enough," she said.

***

"Thanks for spending your Saturday helping me, Trudy." *Mamm* patted Trudy's sleeve on her way back to the stove to load the pressure canner with filled quart jars. They were spending the day on an annual fall chore: canning chunks of beef to be used in her mother's hearty stews and soups. "This job goes a lot faster with both of us working."

"Well, I ought to help." Trudy chopped the meat into uniform pieces. "Seeing as how I plan on being one of the people sitting at your table this winter." Her mother shot her a questioning look. "I think it's time I moved back home, *Mamm*. For good."

"Oh." Vera paused, one jar held aloft with tongs to consider her daughter. "It didn't work out, then? With your friend Eli? We've been wondering."

"*Nee*, it didn't. Turns out he wasn't so interested in me, after all." Trudy did her best to keep her voice even.

It wasn't easy. Those sweet flutters Eli always caused in her stomach had shifted to a sick heaviness. Just hearing his name jolted her and had, ever since that moment, standing at Susie's door, when she'd offered Eli a way out.

And he'd taken it.

If she lived to be a hundred, she didn't think she'd forget how awful that had felt—waiting to see if the man she'd come to love would choose her or not.

She'd held her breath hoping what Leah and Abby had said wasn't true. There had been moments, achingly sweet moments like that kiss at the picnic, and when he'd given her the box he'd made, when she'd believed that Eli cared for her, that he'd liked the idea of marrying her.

She'd wanted to believe that. But there on Susie's stoop, when she'd offered him the choice between his freedom and their marriage plans, all he'd said was, *I'm sorry.*

"*Ach*, I'm sorry," *Mamm* was saying now, too. "I liked him and his little girl very much. But if Eli isn't the *mann* for you, maybe Susie could—"

Trudy shook her head. "I don't think so, *Mamm*."

"Ah." Her mother nodded slowly, her face creasing with sympathy. "Well, sometimes things aren't meant to be. *Gott* knows best."

"*Ja*, He knows best." Trudy was trying to take comfort in that.

She filled another jar and added a spoonful of salt. Everything would get easier, she told herself, as time went by. She had her faith, her loving family, plenty of friends. Surely, after a while she wouldn't feel this empty ache where her hopes used to be. Until that happened, she'd do her best to be cheerful and helpful—like a Good Apple Girl should be.

Although she wasn't sure how cheerful she'd feel, seeing Eli twice a day when he brought Leah by and picked her up. Of course, maybe he wouldn't even want her to look after Leah anymore. That possibility put another painful crack in Trudy's battered heart.

It was her own fault. She shouldn't have started thinking of Leah as her own daughter—but she had.

"Oh, wouldn't you know?" Her mother made a frustrated noise. "Somebody's knocking at the front door, and us with all this canning to get done. Go see who it is, Trudy, will you?"

"All right." Trudy set down her knife, and washed her hands at the sink, wondering wearily who the visitor would turn out to be. Friends and family always came to the back door, and most wouldn't have bothered knocking at all.

Wiping her still-damp hands on her green work dress, Trudy reached for the doorknob. She hoped whoever it was wouldn't be hard to get rid of. *Mamm* was right; they had a lot of work to do yet.

She opened the door. *"Gut mar—"* The polite greeting died in her throat.

Eli stood in the brittle November sunshine, his eyes shadowed under the brim of his hat. A sharp breeze blew past him into the warm house, flapping his coat and making goose bumps pop up on her bare arms, where the sleeves of her dress had been folded up to protect them from today's messy work.

"Eli. What are you doing here?" Trudy whispered.

He lifted his chin, looking at her, his jaw set. "Asking if you'd like to go for a buggy ride with me."

"A buggy ride." She repeated the words mechanically. "But, why—"

"What a nice idea!" Trudy turned to see her mother standing behind her. *Mamm* studied Eli with a narrow-eyed interest. "Go ahead, Trudy, if you'd like to. I can manage the rest of the canning on my own, and it's a fine day for a ride. A little chilly, though, so take your shawl." She studied Eli thoughtfully. "We've had a long mild fall, but I sense a big change coming. Don't you?"

Eli kept his eyes on Trudy's. "Could be," he said. "I guess we'll find out soon enough."

"I guess we will." Vera smiled, took Trudy's shawl off the peg by the door and handed it to her—along with a not-so-gentle nudge. "Off you go, Trudy. Have a nice time."

The door clicked shut, and Trudy found herself standing outside with Eli. She wrapped her shawl around herself as tightly as she could and repeated her question. "Eli, what are you doing here?"

"Give me the ride, Trudy." He looked out to the drive

where his horse was waiting patiently. "One buggy ride. Please. And I'll do my best to answer that question."

What could she say to that? "All right."

Chapter Fifteen

When they reached the buggy, Eli offered his hand to steady her as she climbed in. Trudy hesitated a moment before placing her hand in his. His fingers closed around hers, rough with callouses, warm and strong. Her knees promptly went weak, and even with his help, she needed two tries to boost herself up into her seat.

"That wind's sharp, especially when you're moving. Here." He pulled a blanket out of the back, and handed it to her. Then he cleared his throat. "This is for you, too."

He reached back into the back floorboard and pulled out a bouquet of flowers, daisies, both white and yellow, mixed with glossy ferns and wrapped in green tissue.

Trudy drew in a sharp, shocked breath. She'd never known any woman to get a bouquet like this—well, no Amish woman. The *Englisch* women she'd worked for had received them from their husbands sometimes, but Plain men didn't usually give such gifts. The only flowers her *mamm* ever had were the ones she grew herself in the garden.

She squeezed the damp stems in her hands, reassuring herself that she wasn't dreaming. "Eli, they're beautiful. And daisies! In November!"

He glanced at her as he settled into his seat. His cheeks

were red but whether from the cold or from embarrassment, she couldn't tell. "I didn't grow them. I only bought them."

Hope and joy rose up in her heart. "*Ja*, I know. But this is… It's real kind of you. Eli, I—"

"Trudy—" he shot her a desperate glance as he turned the buggy onto the two-lane highway that ran in front of her parents' home "—can we not talk? I mean, not yet. I've got some things to say to you, and I'm going to need my wits about me to say them. I can't do that and drive on this highway at the same time. Let me get us somewhere quiet."

Trudy glanced down at the daisies, their petals fluttering in the chilly wind. Her heart was fluttering, too, and the sick weight in her stomach had vanished. "All right."

He drove only a short distance before turning onto a dirt road that branched off to the right. There were no homes on this road, only a couple of gates leading into pastures belonging to local farmers. Trudy knew this little avenue was a favorite of courting couples because it was quiet and pretty—although, no fellow had ever driven her down it.

Trudy fought a tiny smile. Not until now.

Eli drove to a spot sheltered fairly well from the wind and reined Star to a stop. Then he shifted until he was facing her—and heaved a sigh.

"I'm going to mess this up," he warned her.

"I wouldn't be so sure about that. You're doing pretty well so far. I really like the flowers, Eli."

"I'm glad." He cleared his throat. "I started to get roses. The lady at the flower store said red roses were what most *Englischer* men bought, and I looked them over, but—" He shook his head. "The ones she had didn't look real. They had long stems and were closed up tight, and they had no smell at all. So I looked over the other flowers she had, and those daisies..." His cheeks went a shade darker. "They reminded me of you."

"They did?" Trudy's heart melted.

"*Ja.* Not so fancy, you know, more ordinary—"

"Ordinary?" Trudy couldn't help laughing. Trust Eli to think *ordinary* was a compliment.

"Was that the wrong thing to say? It was, wasn't it?" He made a frustrated noise. "I told Susie I'd ruin this if I had to do much talking. That was why she told me to start off with flowers. Nice ones, she said. I should have gotten the roses."

"*Nee.*" She could barely get the word out. "The daisies are perfect. It's just—never mind." Something he'd said finally registered. "You talked to Susie?"

"*Ja.* I went to see her yesterday, and I asked her to help me figure out how to change your mind about marrying me. She sat me down right there in the bakery kitchen and we had a talk. Or she talked. She had plenty to say, let me tell you." He looked down at his boots. "According to her, I've been going about this courtship business all wrong. Susie said she didn't blame you for shutting that door in my face. She said if I couldn't tell you how I felt, I'd better get busy showing you. And she had a lot of ideas. Those flowers were just the start of it. There was something else, too."

He reached into the back of the buggy again, this time coming up with a small item wrapped in a soft cloth. He removed the wrapping to reveal the little wooden box.

"I gave this to you before. I'd like you to take it back. I made it for you, special, out of maple."

"Because of my hair." She smiled at the memory.

"*Ja*, because of that. And I carved in the pears because you were picking pears that day we met." He flashed a quick look at her. "Maybe that wasn't such a *schmaert* idea. I wasn't so polite that day. But Susie said that wasn't why you wouldn't keep it. She said you gave it back because you didn't think my heart was in it. The courtship, I mean," he amended. "Not the box." He made an exasperated noise. "I'm saying this wrong."

"You're doing better than you think," Trudy assured him softly. "Keep going."

This time, he didn't look down. His eyes held hers, the worry softening out of his face. "I like it when you smile," he said.

He set the box on the seat between them and gathered her hands in his. "It was easier for me to make that box than to tell you how I felt. That I thought your hair was real pretty and that I was thankful for the day I met you. I've just never been so *gut* with people, Trudy. Until Leah came along, the only time things felt…right…to me was when I was alone, working in my shop. Maple and hickory and oak…those things I understand. I see the good in them, and I know how to bring it out. Vernon complains that I'm slow making things, that I make simple jobs too hard, but he doesn't fuss too much. I build slow, that's true. But I build to last."

He drew in a breath and squeezed her fingers. "I've worked with wood since I was a boy, but I'm new at loving. I think it's pretty much the same for me, though. I don't love easy, and I sure don't love quick. But my love will last us, Trudy. I can't promise I won't say things wrong sometimes. Do things wrong. I'll likely hurt your feelings and make you mad, no matter how hard I try not to. But the love will be there underneath all my mistakes, always." He reached up to trace her cheek with his finger. "I can't give you much, maybe, but I can give you that. A love strong enough to build a life around, to build a family on. If," he went on—a hint of hope in his eyes, "you're done shutting doors in my face."

* * *

Trudy's heart was so full that it took her a minute to answer him. "I didn't like shutting that door in your face, Eli. The truth is, I was hoping you wouldn't let me shut it. Or that, at least, you'd open it back up. But then you didn't."

"I didn't know, Trudy. If I'd known, if I'd had any idea you felt that way, I'd have kicked the thing down."

She smiled a little. And hesitated, looking from the daisies in her lap to the carved box resting on the buggy seat.

This was enough, she assured herself. Here this man sat, saying things sweeter than anything out of her books, a man she loved so much that she wasn't sure her heart could beat without him. It should be enough. If she pressed him now, if she asked him the question lurking in the back of her heart, she knew he'd answer her honestly. And she might find out something she didn't want to know.

But Susie would say that sometimes you had to gather up your courage and ask the hard questions—even when you were afraid of the answers.

Maybe especially then. Trudy took a deep breath.

"After I read what Abby said in that letter, I wanted you—I needed you—to have the choice to leave the door closed, if that's what you wanted." She took another steadying breath. "Why did she write that, Eli? That you were being forced to get married to a woman you didn't love?"

He shook his head. "That's not what she said. I know because I've read the letter a hundred times. She said she didn't *want* me to be forced. Abby doesn't know me so well anymore, so she only remembers how I felt in the past, before I knew you. Back then I couldn't imagine ever wanting to get married." He looked up at her then. "But that's because I couldn't imagine you, Trudy. I couldn't imagine such a woman existed in the world. You're so—" He stopped, apparently searching for the right word.

"Ordinary?" She couldn't help it, but she smiled when she said it.

"Ja," he said softly. When she laughed, he added hastily. "It's not a bad thing, being ordinary. Not the way I meant it." He reached out and touched one of the delicate white petals. "Daisies are everyday flowers. Pretty, you know, but sturdy. They come back every year once you plant them, faithful-like, and they're cheerful, too. My *mamm* used to plant daisies in any corner that needed a little light. She said they brightened up any place you put them." He paused. "That's what I meant, calling you ordinary. Because you're like that for me. The world—my world—it's just brighter wherever you are. Won't you marry me, Trudy? Please?"

She looked at him, his face tense and earnest. He looked desperately worried and hopeful at the same time, and his hands shook a little, holding hers tightly as he waited for her answer.

This moment could have come straight out of one of her books—or her daydreams. Of course, when she'd imagined a man asking her to be his wife, she'd always imagined it happening in spring. A beautiful warm day, with flowers blooming everywhere, and her with her nicest dress on—not an old work dress with a stain on the skirt.

She'd never imagined it happening on a chilly day in November, sitting in a buggy on a dirt road, the fields around them already browning in anticipation of winter. But none of that mattered. She glanced down at the daisies and smiled. Eli had brought the spring with him.

She had a feeling that—for her—he always would.

How could she find the right words to tell him that? To explain to him how much he meant to her? Her whole body was full of such joy that she could hardly sit still, much less think straight.

She wanted to tell him how much she loved him—how she'd love him more, day after day, year after year as their lives together unfolded. She wanted to tell him what a blessing he was, how *Gott* had answered her prayers more generously than she could ever have imagined on the day He sent Eli Mast in search of a matchmaker.

She wanted to tell him all those things. But she just… couldn't. The feelings were so big and so beautiful that no words she could think of even came close. She'd never felt this much at a loss for words before. Maybe she and Eli had more in common than she'd thought.

But now she'd have a lifetime to find ways to tell him all those things. And that was good because it would take her at least that long—maybe longer.

"Trudy?" His voice was so ragged that she looked up in surprise. "Aren't you going to say anything? Are you going to marry me or not?"

"Oh!" She blinked. "Oh, *ja*! *Ja*, I'll marry you, Eli. Of course, I will! The way I love you, I couldn't do anything else!"

Breath rushed out of him in a long and heartfelt sigh of relief. "*Ach*, I'm glad, but you really shouldn't twist a fellow's heart like that! The longer you went without talking, the more worried I got that you didn't care for me at all, and that all my hopes about marrying you were about to come to nothing, and—" He stopped, looking at her reproachfully. "Why are you laughing? It's not funny. I'd never do such a thing to you."

When Trudy only laughed harder, Eli looked confused. Then realization dawned in his eyes, and his mouth quirked up in a rueful grin.

"All right, fair enough," he admitted sheepishly. "But you have to admit, I never did it on *purpose*."

And he leaned over to silence her helpless giggles with his kiss.

Epilogue

The following March, Trudy Mast walked out of her father's biggest work shed, freshly married to the man of her dreams. Smiling from ear to ear, she walked across the yard toward the house, Eli at her side.

Everything had gone off just right. The early spring weather wasn't trustworthy enough to use the pole barn, as they'd done for her sister's fall weddings. *Mamm* had pointed that fact out more than once, hinting that an autumn wedding would be far more sensible. But since Eli had been just as horrified as Trudy at the prospect of waiting so long, they'd settled on clearing out the largest enclosed shed for the church service and having the meal in the house.

It all worked out, but it hadn't been easy, especially since Trudy and Eli had insisted on doing as much of the preparation as they could themselves. However now, looking at her parents' familiar living room, transformed with long tables covered with white cloths, Trudy smiled. Their hard work had been well worth it.

Daisies were everywhere, sprinkled on the special dishes she'd collected and arranged in sweet bouquets on each table. Pretty polished apples were heaped in bowls on each table as well, a detail that had puzzled her sisters.

Why apples? Daisies are just right for a spring wedding, but apples do better for fall.

Trudy had only smiled and insisted on the apples, her own private joke.

She took her seat at her daisy-bedecked Eck, the bridal table, thankful that their community's tradition sent the newlyweds in first before the rest of the first-seating guests came in. Teenaged helpers, overseen by Susie, bustled about, shooting Trudy and Eli quick smiles, but politely keeping their distance so that the newly married couple could have a few private words before they were joined by their closest friends and family.

She smiled at Eli—her husband now, for the rest of their lives. "Wasn't our wedding just perfect?" she breathed happily.

"It was awful." Eli's cheeks were still ruddy with embarrassment as he took his seat next to her. "So many people and standing in front of everybody and all. But at least the church part's done. How long until the rest of this mess is over with?"

Trudy chuckled, but Susie paused on her way past the Eck to wag a teasing finger at Eli. "Mess? What a thing for a groom to say about his own wedding supper! You might at least give poor Trudy ten minutes of happiness before she realizes what a mistake she made."

For a second, Eli looked stricken, but then his face cleared. "Well, according to the bishop, she *is* my wife now, so I guess she's stuck with me, mistake or not."

Susie clucked her tongue. "Eli Mast, you're enough to put me off matchmaking for life."

But there was an affectionate twinkle in Susie's eye as she spoke, and as the older woman bustled away, her gaze lingered thoughtfully on sad-eyed Lydia Riehl, who was helping elderly Mattie Kauffman to her seat.

Gut, Trudy thought with the expansive generosity of a delighted bride. She'd not seen the young beekeeper smile for almost three years, not since her fiancé passed away so tragically. Hopefully, Susie would soon find Lydia a husband, too, although, whoever the man was, he couldn't be half so wonderful as her Eli. She sighed again.

"What do you keep sighing for? Do you really wish you'd said no to marrying me, Trudy?" Eli asked, a worry line forming between his eyebrows.

"Hmm." Trudy tossed him a teasing look, pretending to consider the question. Then she laughed. "Not a bit, Eli. I'm the happiest woman in the world!"

"Gut." He smiled. "I'm relieved to hear it. Susie had me worried for a minute. Although," he added with a wink, "I should've reminded her that you'd be as much to blame as me, seeing as how you proposed to me first."

"I did, didn't I?" Trudy answered absently, watching Leah smiling and chattering with her new *kossins*. The little girl caught Trudy's eye and waved enthusiastically before allowing *Mammi* Vera to lead her to her seat.

"Leah looks happy," Trudy said with some satisfaction. "*Mamm* says she's fitting right in with the other children, and—" She stopped and frowned. "Wait a minute. What do you mean, you should have *reminded* Susie? You didn't tell Susie I proposed to you. Did you?"

Eli's smile faded, and the worry line reappeared. "Ah..." He shifted uneasily on his chair.

She drew in a sharp horrified breath. "Oh, Eli."

"It sort of came out that day I went to see her in the bakery. I was afraid I'd lost you for good. I wasn't thinking straight, and you know how I am. Always saying something

I shouldn't. And Susie asks a lot of questions, Trudy. I don't see how any man could keep a secret around her for long. But what difference does it make? So long as we ended up married in the end, who cares who asked first?"

Exasperated, Trudy made a face. "You think that because you're a man. When a man proposes to a woman, people think it's sweet. But when a woman proposes to a man, folks think it's funny."

"*Ach*. I... I didn't know. I'm sorry, Trudy," he said.

"Well..." Trudy considered. He did look sorry, and this wasn't really his fault. After all, he'd only told Susie the truth. "I don't suppose it matters. It's just...people have been making fun of me for years. Joking about how badly I wanted to get married and all that. Now I finally am married, but whenever our names come up, all anybody will remember is that I proposed to you instead of the other way around."

More people were filing into the room. Besides, she couldn't let such a silly thing ruin this special day. "Never mind, Eli. What's done is done. If folks want to talk about us, let them talk."

"Oh, folks are going to talk about us, Trudy," he said fiercely. "They'll talk plenty. Because I'm going to see to it." He picked up the box he'd made for her, holding it between them. "They'll talk about us for years, all the way down to when our children's children are trying to decide who gets this box I made for you after we're both gone. And you know what they'll say?"

For a second, Trudy just stared at him, at the strong, lean lines of his face, the shock of dark hair falling over his forehead, at the love and determination gleaming in his eyes.

As of fifteen minutes ago, this amazing man was officially her husband, and now he was sitting at their bridal table talking about their grandchildren? How in the world could any woman be expected to talk sensibly after that?

But he was waiting for her to answer his question, so she gave it a try.

She took the box gently from his hands. "I expect they'll say 'What a fine craftsman our *grossdaddi* was. Look at how beautifully he made this, how well it's lasted all these years. No wonder our smart *grossmammi* chased the poor man down until he married her.'"

He smiled at her—the special smile that always caught at her heart. "*Nee*, Trudy. You're wrong. They'll only talk about how much I loved you. Time will chisel the rest of it away and polish up our story until only the truest part shines through. Old Eli was an odd fellow, they'll say, but one thing's for certain sure. No man ever loved a woman better than he loved his Trudy. They'll talk about how I brought you daisies even in the middle of winter because they made you smile. They'll talk about how often I held your hand and how I was never happier than when I was with you. And if they have any sense, they'll pray and ask *Gott* to give them a marriage like ours for themselves. *Ja*," he said with a nod. "That's what folks will talk about when they think of you and me, Trudy. In the end, that'll be what they remember."

Before Trudy could answer, their side-sitters arrived to take their seats at the Eck. She threw Eli an agonized glance, but all the loving words she wanted to say would have to wait until later. Until they were alone.

Trudy set the carved box down in its spot of honor and gave it an affectionate pat. "Well, I hope you're right," she whispered.

"I am," Eli whispered back. "I may not have read so many books as you about romance and all, and maybe I don't understand people so well, but I'm right about this. You just wait and see."

And, as it turned out, he was.

* * * * *

Dear Reader,

Welcome back to the Amish community of Hickory Springs, Tennessee, where life is a little slower, a little sweeter—and where romance blooms around every corner!

As usual, we find our matchmaker friend Susie Raber smack dab in the middle of a very unlikely romance. On the one hand, she has Trudy Schwartz, a hopeless romantic who's eager to trade in her career as a nanny to be a wife and mother. And on the other, she's dealing with Eli Mast, a solitary carpenter who never planned to marry—and wouldn't be considering it now if the bishop had given him any other choice. I guess it's a good thing Susie specializes in hard-to-match couples, because she's sure got her work cut out for her with these two!

Enjoy this third visit to Hickory Springs, my friend! I hope we'll make many more trips to this very special town and watch Susie arrange many more happily-ever-afters!

In the meantime, I'd love to stay in touch! Head over to laurelblountbooks.com and sign up to be a part of my favorite bunch of folks—my beloved newsletter subscribers! Every month, I share photos, book news and gotta-try-it recipes. You can also find me on Facebook, Instagram and Bookbub, and, of course, you can always write to me at laurelblountwrites@gmail.com. I look forward to hearing from you!

Much love,
Laurel

Get up to 4 Free Books!

We'll send you 2 free books from each series you try PLUS a free Mystery Gift.

FREE Value Over **$25**

Both the **Love Inspired®** and **Love Inspired® Suspense** series feature compelling novels filled with inspirational romance, faith, forgiveness and hope.

YES! Please send me 2 FREE novels from the Love Inspired or Love Inspired Suspense series and my FREE gift (gift is worth about $10 retail). After receiving them, if I don't wish to receive any more books, I can return the shipping statement marked "cancel." If I don't cancel, I will receive 6 brand-new Love Inspired Larger-Print books or Love Inspired Suspense Larger-Print books every month and be billed just $7.19 each in the U.S. or $7.99 each in Canada. That is a savings of 20% off the cover price. It's quite a bargain! Shipping and handling is just 50¢ per book in the U.S. and $1.25 per book in Canada.* I understand that accepting the 2 free books and gift places me under no obligation to buy anything. I can always return a shipment and cancel at any time by calling the number below. The free books and gift are mine to keep no matter what I decide.

Choose one: ☐ **Love Inspired Larger-Print** (122/322 BPA G36Y)   ☐ **Love Inspired Suspense Larger-Print** (107/307 BPA G36Y)   ☐ **Or Try Both!** (122/322 & 107/307 BPA G36Z)

Name (please print)

Address   Apt. #

City   State/Province   Zip/Postal Code

Email: Please check this box ☐ if you would like to receive newsletters and promotional emails from Harlequin Enterprises ULC and its affiliates. You can unsubscribe anytime.

Mail to the Harlequin Reader Service:
IN U.S.A.: P.O. Box 1341, Buffalo, NY 14240-8531
IN CANADA: P.O. Box 603, Fort Erie, Ontario L2A 5X3

Want to explore our other series or interested in ebooks? Visit www.ReaderService.com or call 1-800-873-8635.

---

*Terms and prices subject to change without notice. Prices do not include sales taxes, which will be charged (if applicable) based on your state or country of residence. Canadian residents will be charged applicable taxes. Offer not valid in Quebec. This offer is limited to one order per household. Books received may not be as shown. Not valid for current subscribers to the Love Inspired or Love Inspired Suspense series. All orders subject to approval. Credit or debit balances in a customer's account(s) may be offset by any other outstanding balance owed by or to the customer. Please allow 4 to 6 weeks for delivery. Offer available while quantities last.

Your Privacy—Your information is being collected by Harlequin Enterprises ULC, operating as Harlequin Reader Service. For a complete summary of the information we collect, how we use this information and to whom it is disclosed, please visit our privacy notice located at https://corporate.harlequin.com/privacy-notice. Notice to California Residents – Under California law, you have specific rights to control and access your data. For more information on these rights and how to exercise them, visit https://corporate.harlequin.com/california-privacy. For additional information for residents of other U.S. states that provide their residents with certain rights with respect to personal data, visit https://corporate.harlequin.com/other-state-residents-privacy-rights/.